PULLING TAFFY

PULLING TAFFY

MATT BERNSTEIN SYCAMORE

suspect thoughts press
www.suspectthoughts.com

Cover image and design by Shane Luitjens/Torquere Creative. Book design by Greg Wharton/Suspect Thoughts Press. Author Photo by Laurie Sirois.

First Edition: March 2003
ISBN 0-9710846-3-7

Library of Congress Cataloging-in-Publication Data

Sycamore, Matt Bernstein.
 Pulling taffy / Matt Bernstein Sycamore.
     p. cm.
 ISBN 0-9710846-3-7 (pbk.)
 1. Gay men—Fiction. I. Title.
PS3619.Y33P85 2003
813'.6—dc21

                                   2002156171

Suspect Thoughts Press
2215-R Market Street, PMB #544
San Francisco, CA 94114-1612
www.suspectthoughts.com

Suspect Thoughts Press is a terrible infant hell-bent to publish challenging, provocative, stimulating, and dangerous books by contemporary authors and poets exploring social, political, queer, and sexual themes.

Acknowledgments

For editorial brilliance: Jon Curley, Jennifer Fink, Lauren Goldstein, Krandall Kraus, Reginald Lamar, zee mandra, Brian Pera, D. Travers Scott, and Andy Slaght.

For support, encouragement, and advice: Ralowe T. Ampu, Erica Berkowski, Erica Berman, Scott Berry, Susie Bright, Gina Carducci, Kara Davis, Erik Eyster, Johanna Fateman, Bob Glück, Chris Hammett, Keith Hennessy, Thea Hillman, Jason, James Johnstone, Jennifer Joseph, Stephen Kent Jusick, KeriOakie, Kris, Kristen, Richard Labonté, Ananda LaVita, Michael Lowenthal, Jane McAndrew, Mark Menke, Keidy Merida, Tony Mueller, Jandy Nelson, Elizabeth Norman, Tracy Quan, Carol Queen, Jonathan Rabinowitz, Kirk Read, Rhani Remedes, Kevin Schaub, Brian Schultz, Jason Sellards, Jess Socket, Karl Soehnlein, Greg Spector, Jenna Stephens, Tristan Taormino, Karen X. Tulchinsky, Eric Von Stein, Steve Zeeland, and anyone else whom I may have inadvertently forgotten.

For turning it out: Ian Philips and Greg Wharton.

To Gay Shame for grounding me.

To my family of choice — you know who you are.

Portions of the novel *Pulling Taffy* first appeared, in different versions, in the following (print and web) magazines and anthologies: *Afterwords, Best American Gay Fiction 3, Best Gay Erotica 2000, Best Gay Erotica 2001, Best Gay Erotica 2002, Black Sheets, Blithe House Quarterly, Evergreen Chronicles, Flesh and the Word 4, I See Gays, Lodestar Quarterly, Queer View Mirror 2, Quickies, Suspect Thoughts,* and *Velvet Mafia.*

The excerpt from "Lenny" by Sam D'Allesandro is reprinted with the kind permission of the literary estate of Sam D'Allesandro.

The excerpt from "Sex Life 1979" by Owen Hill is reprinted with the kind permission of the author.

To Andy for always believing in me

For JoAnne, 1974-1995

PULLING TAFFY

Contents

Walls

Walking Around

We don't get out of the house until 6 p.m., rush to the clinic for our 7 o'clock appointment. They tell me I have crabs, even though a week ago they said I didn't. Gabby's all nerves and a few bumps of coke, waiting for her HIV test results. She turns out negative, we go to Buddha's Delight to celebrate because I'm vegan so we can't go anywhere else.

While we're eating, Gabby sees some van that says Boston Streetworkers, what could that be? I say must be for street*sweeping*. Gabby says they don't sweep the streets in Chinatown. We leave and the van comes around again, men or boys leaning out, driver screams You gay *son of a shit*. Gabby says I *am* a son of a shit. I say me too, we go to Playland and Gabby gets an Absolut Cape Cod that's almost colorless, I get water in a Pocahantas cup. Gabby talks to the owner about buying a wig, this queen comes behind the bar to tell me about her forty-fifth birthday, went out with her friend done up and *no one even blinked*.

We walk to Copley Square where Jason Barrows can barely say hello because now he's straight. Gabby calls Lincoln and Randy for her makeup so she can do the eyebrow thing, I call a trick who paged me two hours ago. Over to the Westin Hotel to use the bathroom, which is packed because everyone's moved there to cruise after the Back Bay Station arrests. I get severe back pain in the Westin lobby and Gabby's strung out or bored.

We go to White Hen after sitting on the steps of the library where I can't paint my nails because it's too dark. And White Hen is definitely the highlight. This boy, seventeen or eighteen, ghetto-style, says why'd you do that shit to your hair, what's up with that shit, that looks fucked up. I say maybe you should put some in your hair. He says what, you look fucked up, he's looking me up and down, are you gay? I say of course I am. He says that's fucking disgusting, he's making a big scene all loud, that's fucking disgusting, you're fucking disgusting. I say a few things that end in honey and he's not too happy, yelling out at me and Gabby as we leave the store, you two are fucking disgusting, God will strike you down, fucking faggots faggot fuckers shitpokers, why you living in *my* world... And of course the butch muscleboy fag behind us in line who looks all scared, doesn't say a word.

On our way to the T and we run into our friend from White Hen again. He's with five or six other guys who act tough and don't speak, look a little uncomfortable but mostly just laugh. Our friend starts making this scene about how he won't get on the train with us, talking to the T-worker, saying they let these faggots on the T? I'm not getting on the train with these faggots. Gabby's scared, I'm filled with anger and adrenaline and scared too but mostly just disgusted. We get on the train, our friend makes a big deal about not using the same door as us but then he stands a few rows away. Gabby says why'd you get on the same car as him, I'm thinking there's only one car but maybe she meant the train, I didn't even think of not getting on the train.

Gabby says you're pushing him on, looks like Gabby's about to cry so I decide not to say anything, which is probably the right choice because this guy just goes crazy, screaming and yelling, all glassy-eyed and sweaty — You fuckin' faggot you look like a dog, you think that looks good? You look like a fuckin'

14

dog, you dog woof woof both of you, which one's the man and which one's the woman—you both women or you with the purse is the woman? Pink and blue hair—who the fuck gave you that idea?

I'm staring through him for a little while then reading and trying to look like I don't care. He's imitating RuPaul, saying *Girlfriend you better work,* chanté chanté, what's his name? *What's his name?* Your fucking dirty assholes, better wipe them off better fucking clean out those assholes. And everyone on the train is silent of course, or worse they're laughing but I'm not looking up really, we get to Park Street where the train ends and he screams *faggots,* then goes down to the Red Line. This woman about our age comes up to us, says I'm really sorry about that, I'm really sorry, I wanted to say something but I couldn't. I think why not but Gabby says well it was too scary. Then another woman comes over, says the same thing, thanks, and they both say I like your hair. And then off of the Lechmere train comes this cute boy who Cookie claims I made out with at the Loft, he gives each of us a soft hard kiss, no idea of what just happened, you girls going out tonight?

We get on the train and everyone's sort of staring. Go to Government Centre, I'm painting my nails on the platform and this woman who we've seen here before sits down next to Gabby and starts blabbing about her small paycheck and waitressing and her boyfriend. And she lives on Webster Street where we live, her neighbor complains about the noise they don't make.

The train comes, she says you can't tell how old anyone is these days, how old are you? Gabby says nineteen, I say twenty-one, the woman says I'm twenty-four—well there is that five years I guess but no one knows, we look young and everyone buys their clothes at Macy's now, I moved from New York to Seattle to Wyoming to Seattle to New Haven, thought I'll get a job in Boston, went to school for film but I need a job before I get a *job*. I fight with my boyfriend and we're loud, called the cops on him once and they took him away for the night so the landlord holds that against us. But we're not loud, just look like we should be loud, don't know anyone so we don't have parties, don't even play loud music, walk around in the apartment at 3 a.m. and the neighbor calls the landlord. Before when I was single I had all these plans, now we like to do nothing and have fun.

Florence and Rose

Florence and Rose aren't drag queens. Still, they might be able to pass: Florence with the Chanel choker and Fendi bag, Hermes scarf which reads Chanel. Rose with the pink-red hair and drawn-in eyebrows that don't quite match. You can almost see them saying *Honey* — these tits are *real*.

Florence and Rose aren't having a lesbian affair, but they've planned well. Sharing finances so they don't have to argue about who's paying, so Florence won't be embarrassed that she, with the Chanel choker, has less to spend than Rose, with the mismatched eyebrows and hair. They argue, but who doesn't?

When Florence isn't wearing heels, Rose is. They agree about one thing: these heels hurt. Make that two things: Matthew shouldn't be hustling. Wait — grandmothers talking with their grandson about hustling? Florence says Matthew, why can't you be a normal homosexual?

The irony for all three of them is different. They walk: Florence in front, Matthew in the middle, Rose in back. They sit by the fountain at the Esplanade and look at the gold, pink, rose of the sun in the water.

Rose guesses it, says Florence can't you tell he was raped? Florence is shocked, Matthew's relieved but tense. Rose is worried: Matthew are you sure you *know* who it is?

Florence's annoyed at Rose: of course he knows who it is. Rose changes the subject: where are we going for dinner?

Florence and Rose love everything about Boston except the homeless people. Someone asks them for change and Rose says I could smell the whiskey on his breath. Florence says oh Rose. Matthew wants to tell them his dream, the homeless woman with her blanket stretched out like floral-print wings. She falls head first, and when Matthew bends to help her, her head is gone.

Family Meals

Rolling corn-on-the-cob into a plate of melted butter, my father smacked his lips then wiped off the grease with a paper napkin, wrinkled the napkin into a tiny ball, and dropped it onto my place mat. My mother licked the grease from the mini-grill. My sister and I ate our salads. When my sister was done, she was done. Girls were allowed to be anorexic, and I hated her for it. I hid the rest of my food in napkins when no one was looking.

When we visited Germany, the carpet everywhere was brown or red, my sister and I ordered *wiener schnitzel*. I tried to vomit in the bathroom, but I wasn't good at bulemia. You know it's anorexia when you see it on tv. But the title was too long for a CBS After-School Special: "Anorexic Closeted Twelve-Year-Old Faggot Buys a Twix Bar, Reese's Peanut Butter Cups, a Three Musketeers, Skittles and Starburst, Takes One Bite of Each and Then Throws Everything into the Trash, Goes Back to School to Wait for His Father."

In Germany, I ended up crying in a park in the rain; my parents couldn't find me but there was nowhere to go. When we got back, Rose said you look like a concentration camp victim, and later she regretted that comment but I was flattered: it meant I was thin.

This happened all the time. When my mother put a whole chicken on my plate, I said I only want one piece. Who eats a whole chicken? My mother told me to eat what I wanted. The chicken never flew away, so one night I counted to five and then dumped it into the trash. Slammed the door to my room on my father slamming against the door. I was *studying*.

Sometimes my father looked like he was about to tell the funniest joke. He turned to me and said *Is that all you're going to eat*? His face got all red and his eyes grew wide and I wanted to grab his wrists until his hands fell off. But I practiced how to look right through his eyes until my face went blank like no one else was in the room; then I'd won.

It was a family meal, everyone was at our house and I was actually eating because Rose cooked. Then my father looked over at my plate and when I looked at him I couldn't make my eyes blank, they were filled with everything I'd ever wanted to vomit out. But he said it anyway, smirked while he was saying it — it became a refrain at the table: *is that all*? I stood up and dropped my plate of food onto the floor. Soon, we wouldn't eat together any more.

Birthday Money

You pound your fists into everyone who wishes they could cry about ice cream. Someone steps on a turtle, they're so slow. "If only there'd been free-range chicken when I grew up..." Financial news: anger doesn't have to be a wall.

The Night That Plays Like Ping-Pong in My Head

I wake up and I've wet my bed, one of my socks is filled with piss, the bathroom floor is soaked. I almost pass out on the bus, come home and sleep for twenty hours. All because of this trick who brought tequila. And I don't even drink tequila. He came over and started chopping limes. I said I'm only gonna have a shot or two, put down that knife. He said I'd never hurt you — you know that, don't you? I said I'm just afraid of knives. He said you can tell by the eyes, look me in the eyes. His eyes were practically glazed over. He poured me a shot, handed me a lime and asked if I had any sea salt. Before I knew it, the bottle was close to empty, I was on the ceiling licking salt off my hand and chewing limes. He tried to stick a hundred-dollar bill up my ass, I went to the bathroom. Came back and the money was gone. I said did you just put that hundred back in your pocket? He said what hundred? At some point he gave back the money, like it hadn't been in my asshole or anything. Then he said I'll give you another hundred if you get hard again. I'd just come in his mouth, and I hate having my dick touched after I come, but for an extra hundred, whatever. I said pour me another shot, and then he was sucking my dick again, before I knew it I was hard. He wanted me to fuck him. I tried, but couldn't stay hard: no big shock. We took a break, he asked me if I'd go to Mexico with him. We'd sit on the beach and drink margaritas all day. I said first you'll have to give me that other hundred. He said you're not charging me by the hour. I said I just got hard. He said yeah, but you didn't fuck me. I looked him in the eyes. He looked away. That's when I got dramatic. I said *look* me in the eyes, and I stared right at him, right at his eyes. He couldn't hold my gaze. I said *the eyes don't lie*, and I kept staring right at him. He got all nervous, kept repeating that I hadn't fucked him, he'd already given me a hundred. I was through. I said listen bitch, you better take out that hundred or I'm not calling you again. He said I don't have another hundred. I said do you think you can work me? I said honey I've been turning tricks since I was fourteen, and I went into the kitchen for effect. Or water. Then I came back, picked up that tequila and took one big swig. I said you and I both know, and I looked him right in the eyes, you and I both know that it's not about money. He reached for the bottle and I pulled it away. I was swinging the bottle in the air, if he'd taken out the money right then, I would have ripped it into shreds.

Walls

When JoAnne died, there was cardboard in my ears, even though I don't know what that means. When you leave cardboard out in the rain, it rots, collapses but doesn't quite disintegrate. Maybe I'm writing about my ears because that's how I found out, Laurie called to say JoAnne's dead and I wanted cardboard in my ears, only it rots, collapses but doesn't quite disintegrate.

Once I kept a burnt piece of toast for a year, in a plastic bag like a fossil. A week before JoAnne died, I went to see the movie *Kids*, which made me walk all the way across Boston to get on a train. Anywhere. The train station was closed. So was the subway — everything in Boston closes. A week before I saw *Kids*, I confronted my father, and *he* screamed at *me*. Someone could have told me that you don't leave rapists in the park, not before dark at least. But it was After Dark, the screensaver that Laurie worked on, before and maybe even when she called me to say JoAnne's Dead: A Screensaver by Berkeley Systems.

Do you know what a screensaver is? It's that annoying thing that flashes on your computer when you leave the keyboard alone. Supposedly it saves the screen from disintegration — I still have the screensavers on my computer that Laurie gave me, before JoAnne died, before I'd ever met JoAnne and before I'd started to see my father under the bed with an axe, behind the curtains.

I told my father to come out from under that bed, I said here's the movie I want you to see: *I May Not Know What You Did Last Summer, but I Know What You Did in the Summers When I Was a Kid*. You made me old enough to be my father. Until I met Laurie, who said your shards match mine, and we broke together. Until I met JoAnne, who said we can spit out the glass and the blood like bubbles.

I left my father in the park, a danger to his own kids but what about the kids in the park? I left my father screaming in the park, because no we could not *discuss* this. I left my father discussing: disgusting.

When I left that park, slowly, because no my father wasn't coming after me, I looked up at the buildings and they blurred me. I wanted to be clearer. I finally found my mother where I'd left her, in the restaurant where the glass door was so clear that my father slammed into it, which could have been an omen.

My mother and I rushed into a cab like we were fleeing Boston or *Kids*, but I was fleeing much more and so was my mother. We went to another park, the one where I made out with a guy as the sun came up and I sucked his dick in the reeds, we were cold but warming each other. On this day it was hot, the Boston summer sweating over us, and my mother and I sat down in the shade.

I started bawling and my mother wanted to touch me but I touched her to tell her not to touch me. And then I gave my mother what I'd written to my father, what he hadn't read yet, what his mother — Rose — would read over and over until she'd call me to say please tell me this isn't what I've read. She said you're destroying people.

The cab driver wanted to take us to the baseball stadium, I said this is no game. My mother read in the park while I looked at the sun in the flowers and thought about taking ecstasy during the day. I watched the guys to see if they were cruising and I even saw someone I knew, my face covered in tears, I smiled hello like an ad for underwater suntan lotion.

My mother finished and looked up, she said this feels so alien. But she'd been gone for a long time and UFOs just weren't going to explain it. When she said he's not homosexual, I remembered *Heathers*, how they find bottled water and they know this guy's gay, but really I was thinking *fuck me gently with a chainsaw*.

Then I gave my mother a private letter, which said I'm not sure what you did in the summers (and springs, falls, and winters), when he fingerfucked me like a new toy. But I know that you took your turn. She said maybe you're right, I used to be very seductive. She didn't say he raped me then bought me, because that was *my* line. She didn't say I raped you then bought you — a new sweater from Bloomingdale's.

She said I need to use the phone, and when we walked through the park I saw the reeds had been chopped down and I felt sick. My mother said you're worrying about the environment at a time like this, and I said no that's where men have sex in the dark — and they cut down the reeds just to stop it — and my mother didn't know what to say. When she got to the phone, she called my father, to see how *he* was doing. We got in a cab, I left my mother several blocks before her hotel. She didn't realize that she'd dropped me off on the Boyblock, where I worked when there wasn't enough work elsewhere.

According to my mother, hustling is a death sentence. I wasn't in the mood for hustling anyway, just cocktails and drugs, honey, drugs. Though when Laurie told me JoAnne died, I lay down like I could become the floor. I thought about where I could go to smash glass, then I got a page and believe it or not I took the call because I needed the money, it actually made me sane.

Laurie and I used to steal pint glasses from all the cafes in San Francisco, then hurl them into the air shaft when we were breaking. Once, I broke the window of our downstairs neighbors' apartment; we didn't like them anyway. But a week after I confronted my parents, I went to see *Kids*, which made me break down, just like and not just like a week later, when Laurie called to say JoAnne's dead. Two days after that, I got on a plane for San Francisco, where JoAnne died, because I was afraid of what might happen if I stayed in Boston.

I went to San Francisco to break glass, didn't expect that it would feel like home. My friends honored my grief and JoAnne's friends honored me like a part of her that was intact, blooming in her backyard. We planted garlic for JoAnne. I told everyone how, when JoAnne and I lived together, we always alternated making a stir-fry for dinner. When I cooked, it was a ginger stir-fry, with lots of green cabbage and scallions. When JoAnne cooked, she used garlic and fresh dill instead of ginger, and red cabbage with onions and cashews.

JoAnne's roommates, Jed and Sugar and Zane, told me that JoAnne used to cook my stir-fry for them. I made them JoAnne's stir-fry, but I couldn't stop looking at the couch where she died, surrounded by candles and flowers, her broken alarm clock, packs of cigarettes. On the couch was a blanket, covered in dirt and twigs, Jed said that's where JoAnne died. I kept thinking JoAnne doesn't want to sit there, and *where is JoAnne*?

JoAnne was dead, and now I can't remember what her room smelled like because I couldn't forget then. Walls splattered with blood, vomit caking the floor. I wanted to get her journals and her photographs before her parents did, alone in her room I was alone. I picked up the ring she used to wear, a cheap gaudy tarnished silver ring — with fake green stones — and it's strange how you can feel people through the objects they wear. I put the ring in my pocket.

Jed and Sugar and Zane took care of JoAnne when she'd vomit and shit uncontrollably, when she'd kick and then shoot up again. We had a memorial in the backyard and I don't know what we said, except that we cried, it was hot and sunny and dry, there were cats there. Inside, we looked at pictures — I didn't recognize the JoAnne they knew. She was so skinny. I knew she'd wasted away, because, high and kicking she'd called me — disgusted — to say people run into me on the street and tell me I look so good. Dying.

But JoAnne didn't die from junk. JoAnne died because the hospital looked at her and said you don't have enough money to need us. She waited eight hours one day and twelve hours the next, finally they admitted her. She had active tb and a bladder infection, they hooked her up to an iv for two days, then gave her Tylenol and said go home. People call it kicking, but JoAnne couldn't even walk; her roommates carried her home. Later that night, Jed found her outside, naked in the grass, and, maybe, laughing. The next day she was dead.

Later, Laurie said JoAnne was okay with dying and I wanted to scream because JoAnne always felt walls built around her, and Laurie felt some of those same walls. Laurie said JoAnne's dead and right away I was crying, then I got a call-waiting click from my mother. I said I can't talk now. She said I've been trying to reach you. I said I'm on the other line with Laurie, I just found out my best friend's dead, and I'm going to have to talk to you later.

My mother called again. She said I don't have anyone to talk to, no one cares how I'm feeling, and I thought she wanted to talk about incest. She said I've been driving on the beltway. I felt like saying I just told you my best friend's dead and you tell me that? But she sounded so vulnerable, pulling me to her. I said that's really good, then she told me I don't want you hustling, and I ended up talking about shit for an hour instead of feeling JoAnne's death.

I flew out to San Francisco, called Laurie from the airport, and she said I'm flying out to Boston. She said my grandmother's dying. Laurie and I met for dinner, she said I know our spiritualities are different, but JoAnne was okay with dying. I wanted to scream, but couldn't—because I came out with Laurie, moved to San Francisco with Laurie, and I'd already yelled at Laurie too much.

JoAnne and I shared our anger like a hug. All my life I'd been told to relax; whenever someone said that I wanted to smack them. I was always afraid that if I relaxed, I'd disappear. I'd be a mushy lump on the sofa, people would say what's that?

JoAnne talked about stealing leather jackets to buy crystal and I talked about doing bumps at work, after an argument, before bed. She'd hold me when I couldn't go into my room because of my father's eyes; I'd hold her while she'd tell me about picturing her father in order to get off. We cried together because we finally could. We taught each other to breathe and to chew, basic skills that we didn't have because we had to survive.

Neighbors

Sexual Community '97

When I heard Robert Glück read, he didn't say, "We were planning to have a baby, I think that's a plumbing term. Jackie Kennedy made anal pleasure famous. In the hospital, she suddenly became lucid and rose to the occasion of her death. She said walk for me."

I pat my backpack until it's flat. Melvin told me about his girlfriend and then he showed me his Blow Buddies card, he said isn't she pretty? But back to the backpack on my lap. This greasy drunk guy with stringy hair on the El before I came out. He was wearing Umbro shorts and he had a hard-on, kept glancing over at me and I kept patting the backpack on my lap.

I remember the first time they chopped down the reeds in the Fens, Boston '95. Well the first time they chopped them down while I was *in* them. *You* know how it is. The orgy room between trees was so crowded that night I couldn't move. Fifty guys pulling their shirts up and their pants down and it was freezing outside but I was in the middle so I was warm.

In Seattle, it just won't get warm. Doesn't get that cold either but seven eight months of rain and dark grates on you. The snowstorm we had got me high, I walked down the street screaming and some guy asked me to help him get his van out of the road. I said I can't push because I don't have any traction, and he gave me his keys, said put it in reverse and then drive.

Owen Hill got it right, "We leaned up against a wall and talked. I hate this and that. I'm getting out of here, I'm bored with the scene. But thinking: I like the way your lips come together when you say certain words... We were standing so close that our sides were touching. I turned to put my arm around him and my chin brushed the padded shoulder of his old coat."

This guy came over to lick my toes and I leaned back and moaned, thought okay how am I doing? But then I got hard, so hard my dick was making wet spots on the outside of my pants, good thing I was wearing corduroys. The guy started grabbing my dick through my corduroys and sucking on my toes. I was shoving my foot into his mouth, gagging him and moaning, real moans now.

When I lived with Laurie all the cabinets in the kitchen were shaking, she said I think there's an earthquake. I said that's just the dryer. Found out the next day that it *had* been an earthquake, but it took me months to remember that we didn't have a dryer. Not even a washing machine.

At Basic Plumbing I got two compliments: you've got a *tight* ass, and, you're *exactly* my type. The first one came from the guy who fucked me while his boyfriend watched. Fucked me hard until his boyfriend came and someone else was sucking my dick but it was all teeth so I pushed his head away, and the other guy was still fucking me and then he came in the condom in my ass, pulled his dick out though I wanted more. Then he said you've got a tight ass. Who gave me the second compliment?

At Basic Plumbing another time this guy was fucking my face, grabbing my neck so hard that I pulled a muscle in my side. Someone else was sucking my dick and he was doing poppers so I didn't have to feel his teeth. And then the first guy came in my mouth, no wait *he* didn't come in my mouth, who did? Anyway, someone came in my mouth and then I felt this sudden sense of sexual community though I can't really explain how. Or why. I'll have to come back to that.

Actually the guy who came in my mouth was outside of Pleasuredome, the worst club in San Francisco, five years and still going strong. It happened in his car, he said *girl* you are one wicked cunty fierce bitch, and then he shot in my mouth. His come was sweet, not bitter like my come. That night he was just the first guy I met in the bathroom. The second guy kept pulling my head up when I leaned over to suck his dick. He said you've got a big dick, girls must like that big dick. Rewind. Fast-forward to the guy who I fucked against the stall wall, but he hadn't done enough crystal to relax.

Ringold Alley after the Stud was another night when I bent over for some guy to fuck me, I said don't come in my ass. He said oh it's too *nice*. Afterwards I was thinking what was I doing getting fucked again without a condom? That was before I started carrying condoms around, at Basic Plumbing I even had lube in a dental floss container, because what good is a condom without dental floss? I still haven't found the right case for the condoms though. Ideas?

At the Stud I was sucking some guy's dick in the bathroom and the bartender came in and watched. That's what they do in sf. In Seattle, Trav got banned from the Cuff for a month, after the bartender caught him getting blown. I think the month is over, though; maybe I'll see Trav at the Cuff tonight. After I finish this. Andee *is* waiting for me.

Sam D'Allesandro writes, "When we fucked it was like there wasn't anyone there just this...big...

fuck moving around on the bed." But also I like two sentences earlier, "His eyes closed like it was all just too powerful to look at." And two sentences later, "The only light was a chartreuse neon coming from outside. And Lenny was so thin, his white skin just tinged to a beautiful pale green in the light."

Back to sexual community. It was after I came a second time, this guy who'd watched me getting fucked started talking to me and then he said wait a second we're not supposed to do that here. I said they might kick us out. And the guy who'd fucked me was holding me and we were in this cramped backroom and someone else was doing poppers and the first guy said you never share your poppers.

Painting My Nails

I started painting my nails after I started sleeping with Chris, his nails were blue and chipped and they made him look even sexier. I painted my thumbnails black, people would say ooh what happened to your—oh. Then I did all black for a while, and after Chris stopped painting his nails I did blue. That was back when it was hard to find blue, I searched all the Woolworths and Walgreens for the right shade—cobalt, brighter than Chris' midnight but still deep.

When I went out with Zeb I was into silver. Then white for a while, but my hair dye would always fuck that up. Then purple and all different blues and then I went crazy trying to find green. This woman at a cafe had just the right shade of emerald, said she got it in Hawaii though that probably just meant down the street, I'm not going to tell you where. Back then, people were secretive about where they got their colors. JoAnne stole my best purple when I lived with her in Seattle, then she moved to San Francisco and we scoured the Mission for orange and magenta, teal. Sat in the kitchen soaking our hands in ice water but fucking up our nails anyway.

I still couldn't find the right green, heard they had it in Providence, RI so I drove right over there. Took about a week to get there but it was worth it, I found the perfect green downtown at a wig store. It looked like dioptase, and if you've seen dioptase then you know what I mean. Otherwise, look it up in a mineral book or ask my grandmother Rose. I got the nail polish and then I moved to Boston because it was the closest place with a subway. That's when the new Manic Panic colors came out—looked all bright in the bottle but painted on dull. I found La

Rosa shiny neon yellow at a nail salon in East Boston. Then I left Boston because my green got all sticky, and JoAnne died in San Francisco; I didn't want her parents to get the purple.

What do you do when your best friend dies? I went back to San Francisco, just when Hard Candy came out with colors to fiend for, but they were twelve dollars. I mean, I'd gotten used to splurging on two or three-dollar bottles, but twelve was stretching it a little too far. And they kept Hard Candy behind the counter, I couldn't just slip it into my pocket. Then came Urban Decay: paint your nails to match the bags drawn under your eyes. By the time I got to Seattle, nail color was the rage, even the hip straightboys were painting their nails.

I got over it and then I got over being over it, today I've got silvery teal with magenta holographic glitter painted on top, looks like something you'd see on the walls at a rave. Chris has this habit of waking up in the middle of the night screaming like he's just been tortured, he gasps and throws his body upright. That's what happened when he and Zeb were staying with me, Chris started screaming and that gave me one of the most intense flashbacks I've ever had. I'm talking incest, not acid. Went into the bathroom and I couldn't look up because I was afraid of what I'd see in my eyes. My father was behind the shower curtain and in the walls and in my skin. I was sitting on the floor in the bathroom and I didn't know who I'd be when I walked out the door. My nails saved me, my father wasn't in my nails and I thought okay I'll just be the one who sits naked on the floor in the loony bin, crying and staring into my nails.

Neighbors

Andee says I'm obsessed with tweakers, but I swear I can hear them chopping lines. I know that sound. The other night it went on for fifteen minutes, I mean that's a lot of lines. The tweakers have these parties that start around 4 a.m. — when I'm about to go to bed — and when I wake up the party's still going on. They just got a dog, and they put the dog out on the roof that connects their building to mine every time it has to shit, and the shit just stays out there with their discarded weight bench and a broken bike, and a kitchen knife that's kind of scary because it's always shiny. Once in a while, the tweakers get motivated enough to sweep the shit off the roof, into the courtyard of my building, which might have been a sculpture garden at one point.

Every few days, the tweakers get into these screaming fights and I can't tell whether someone's getting beaten. One time it got to be too much, I leaned out my window and shouted *is this a tv movie*? A few days later, the cops came by the tweakers' apartment, probably someone in my building called them. But that didn't stop the tweakers, the next night they were having another party and lining up to vomit in the bathroom. Then when I woke up they were arguing again.

Usually I get all annoyed when the tweakers keep me up, but last night they were playing an incredible mix, so I got out of bed and started dancing. I can still hear the beat in my head. I wanted to yell down and ask them who it was, but all their blinds were closed.

All Faggots Are Fuckers

I meet him at Basic Plumbing, when we finally touch there's a charge to it. He kisses me and I suck his tongue into my mouth, hold onto his neck with my hands. His tongue is pierced, he keeps sliding it up against the roof of my mouth and then he grabs my head and our tongues reach deep into each other's throats. He pulls my shirt off then slides his hands all over my chest while I hold him against the wall, right at the hips. He runs his hands over my face, usually I freak about that because I think I'm gonna break out. But this time it turns me on, like he's blind and trying to know me.

We jerk each other off in the corner of the backroom. People are watching and on most nights I'd be watching them too, but this time I don't even notice anyone else until after I come. It's so hot in there that when we're done it feels like we're covered in come, not just sweat. I lean up against him and we start kissing again. I ask him if he wants to go over to my house and take a shower. We walk home in the rain, make out in the shower. Water gets in my contacts but it feels okay. He asks me if he can wash my face, I've never let anyone do that before. My body, sure, but not my face. It feels so intimate. I wash his face too and then I make tea.

We hold each other on the sofa and then go to bed. I can't really sleep because I've taken too many herbal energy pills and only half a Valium, but it feels good to have his arms around me. At some point in the morning I hear him putting on his clothes and that's cool, then he goes into the bathroom, and then I hear the door to my apartment open and close. All the sudden I'm wired. I get out of bed, look around and I don't see his number or even a note. I mean, all I wanted was a kiss goodbye or thanks or see you later. Anything but nothing.

Shoes Don't Work

The gaps in your feet like asphalt marks. Acid rain.
He isn't listening to anything reasonable, so you try
a kiss on the kneecap and his groin responds. *¿Como
'stas?* Rent control works. When it rains, you cover
your head, swamps in your shoes.

Earwax

You put your hands over his ears until you can feel a pulse, like his heart beating in his head, but somehow you know it's his brain pushing out. He says it's been a while. You put your arms around him and nibble at his ears, up and down until he giggles. You start licking his cheeks and spitting into his ears until his face is dripping with saliva and he pushes you onto your back and spits on you, laughing. You lay there remembering the first time you got fucked, you were recovering from speed and you told the guy about that but not about the first time. Feeling you were much too old for first times, except the first person who you trusted: Laurie falling apart with and without you. You said it's been a while. You knew it would hurt but you didn't know you'd feel like you were burning up, OPEN THE WINDOW. The guy said we can do something else but you said no, glad that it was happening but scared by the look in his eyes and sad the next day when it felt like he was in China. Now you want to suck the wax out of this guy's ears until he's ready to come, wave after wave into your throat and when you can't take it anymore, standing up to vomit into his mouth. He's laughing and you squeeze him against you. You're hard again but you want to fall asleep in his arms and so you switch places.

Narcissus

I'm modeling for a painter, she puts me in this crazy position—staring at my reflection in the mirror on the floor—but also I have to face the camera so she can see my eyes. Plus, I'm supporting my body weight with my hands, and my shoulders are starting to ache. Her camera stops working; she gives me some tea made from poppy flowers so I'm okay with waiting, staring at myself in the mirror and making faces.

We try again, same position: perfect. Six shots and then her camera stops working again. I ask her about the poppy tea, where to find the poppies, how to make it. She says you boil it for forty-five minutes then cook it down for another forty-five like you're making a sauce. Because it tastes awful. Says she'll give me a poppy from her garden so I'll know what to look for.

When I get home I'm feeling kind of out of it, wired but unable to drag myself off the floor. Then I start getting these shooting pains that go from the base of my back to my shoulders, up through my neck and into my head. My stomach feels like it's going to break out of my body. I run water for a bath because I don't know what else to do. Then Andee stops by and I'm quite a scene, sitting on the rocking chair moaning, head in my hands.

I start feeling nauseous, go into the bathroom and sit on the floor by the toilet. That makes me more nauseous because my bathroom smells like piss. It's smelled that way ever since the toilet flooded, Chris says you just can't get the smell of urine out of a floor. I can't vomit, just sit by the toilet looking at the pubic hairs embedded into the piss stains on the floor.

I stumble out of the bathroom in these running shorts I use as underwear that barely cover my dick, I'm probably scaring Andee. I lay down in my bed and can't think of what to do. I want to take a bunch of Valium and pass out, but I'm afraid I'll just vomit the Valium up. And I only have about ten left—don't want to waste them. The pain reminds me of that time I did mushrooms with Laurie and we thought they were poisoned because my body became a rock; I was screaming while Laurie massaged my back. I thought I was gonna die, just hoped Laurie would call the ambulance. Eventually I passed out.

I'm talking to Andee: do you think this is food poisoning, or do you think I pinched a nerve from modeling? Or do you think it's the V8 they put in the tea? Andee isn't saying much, just kind of looking at me like he's on the Mir space station. I get in the bath and Andee goes outside to smoke a cigarette. I can't lie down in the tub because then I feel too nauseous; I don't want to choke on my own vomit like a woman in my high school did when she drank Everclear straight, I don't think she died but someone did. I sit in the tub, try to look down at my reflection in the water but I can't see much. Guess the water would have to be darker. I get out of the bath and actually that's when I'm wearing the running shorts so maybe that's when I scare Andee or maybe he's already scared or maybe none of this scares him.

I ask Andee if he can make me some tea. Then I go back into the bathroom and finally I vomit, five or six times in waves of two. I think I see little poppy flowers.

Sky in My Eyes

From cobalt to powder blue in seconds. I'm admiring the angle of the holes in his t-shirt against each hair poking out, though really we're not that close. A paper cup rolls down the sidewalk and I try not to breathe: he might hear me.

Bending down to pick up his sunglasses, he's practically moving into my hands, which don't work. Nothing heals. He. Sucks. Everybody's watch is broken. I want to tell him: I found the keys to my landlord's apartment. Let's fuck.

My First Date

I'm late of course. I meet Jeffrey at C.C. Slaughter's, where all the tweakers go for cocktails at 6 a.m. It's called C.C. Attle's now, but no one calls it that. Jeffrey's wearing a motorcycle jacket and a beanie, which is funny because the other night he looked flat-out preppy. We kiss hello, he says I hope you don't mind, I'm with a bunch of rather loud people. I say don't worry.

We go outside and jump into this Jeep Explorer with four drunk thirty-something Bon Marché queens. The jeep is all over the road and Jeffrey's nervous, I'm confused. We pass the BMW store and two of the queens are joking about their BMW at home, or at least I think they're joking. We get to Kid Mohair but it's closed, one of the queens can't believe it. He keeps saying whatever happened to Merlot Mondays, what's there to do in Seattle on a Monday?

Nothing. We go to R Place, and two cops — in full uniform — are drinking at the bar. I feel like I just stepped into an ad for the We're Just Like You campaign. Jeffrey says are you okay? I say I'm fine, and I smile.

Turns out one of the queens is straight. He's looking me up and down, he says wait, are you a girl or a boy? He's in hysterics. He says I just figured out you're a boy, I just figured out Mattilda's a boy. He's giggling and I'm smiling because sometimes I'm so friendly, it's absurd. He says how do I know what's down there? I say you'll just have to trust me.

Jeffrey says Paul, you're out of line, but Paul's off to cruise the bathroom. Jeffrey says he's bordering on offensive. I say oh it doesn't bother me. Jeffrey keeps looking me in the eyes and saying sweet things. That's when I realize this must be a date. I'm confused. I smile.

We talk about San Francisco and how we used to do crystal and dead friends and clubs and fashion victims. It's kind of romantic. He's a little too normal but he's had a life. I don't tell him I'm a whore—I'm not in the mood for that conversation: a what?

Jeffrey lives in Olympia, he's staying the night with one of the queens, the one who actually works at the Bon. His friend leans over and says are you going to my place or his? We blush. Jeffrey says well, we haven't gotten to that point yet, and his friend turns around.

I smile. Jeffrey smiles. I say I don't think I want to sleep with you tonight. He says I understand. I smile. I say tonight I'm just not really in the mood. He says I understand, and we go back to talking about San Francisco and crystal and fashion victims. Jeffrey walks me home.

How Faggots Meet

If It's 7:30 p.m.

Then it's time for Andee to get up. I left the house early today—3:30 p.m.—and I just loved my full hour of daylight, even though it wasn't sunny of course. I call Andee and she's still in bed. I've gotten sketchier than usual, all sugar and a stomachache, though I'm not freaked out about it. Andee picks me up and I've bought plants which I stuff in his car and we're off. Where are we going? QFC: Andee needs some food though I sure don't. They don't have bulk candy, ginger cookies, or corn muffins, so I get a gallon of spring water. By this time I'm working my sugar high/low, and Andee tells me I'm scaring her, which I take as a compliment. I'm loving my 83¢ water and Andee hasn't eaten. Are we going dancing? Okay. Andee eats in the car because he bought meat, I go up to my apartment and eat the ice cream I bought earlier. My stomach feels warped—I don't usually eat dairy or sugar, so I drink some apple cider vinegar, which grounds me just a little. Then I take a B-complex tablet and mix up a potion of spirulina for energy, stevia for hypoglycemia, melissa for depression, yohimbe for lack of sex drive, ginseng for my kidneys. It looks like sea foam only greener. Andee makes a face. Half of my potion and I'm feeling fierce, Andee's looking at my books and I'm describing all the ones he doesn't want to read. I eat and start to feel like shit, so I take a shower and do yoga while Andee waits. She says we're not gonna get there 'til 1. I say I'm almost ready. We leave at 1. Get there and there's no cover or at least no one at the door, the music isn't jungle or house like they said when we called. It's trip hop with too much funk, and we're the only queers of course. The jungle beat starts in and I'm on the dance floor, Andee's watching. The dj's working me, though there definitely isn't any house going on. The music gets harder but there's no one to dance with. I work it out and then it's over, Andee says he'll meet me outside. I get water and put my layers on, look in the mirror. Andee's smoking. I say I wish there were somewhere to get tea, I don't feel like going home. I think of going to Basic Plumbing, but there are never any cute boys there, and I don't want sex anyway, just want something more to do. We go to my building and the Christmas lights are playing music.

How Faggots Meet

On my way back from the co-op, I see this boy with fluorescent green pants walking towards me, I'm thinking who's *she*? When he gets closer, he looks me right in the eyes and we smile across the street at each other. I picture him following me home, I ask him up for a drink, we make out until both of our necks are sore. But then he keeps walking—I can't very well follow him because I've got about fifty pounds of groceries. I go home and drop off my bags, then run out to pick up a package around the corner, and there he is at Coffee Messiah, green pants and all. He's sitting with two women at a table outside. As I walk past, one of the women says that doesn't sound like how you usually flirt.

I get my package and walk back up past the cafe, look the boy with green pants in the eyes and say haven't I seen you three times already? One of the women laughs but he just looks confused, so I say I like your pants, and I keep walking. I bring the package back to my apartment and then I think well if I've seen him three times I might as well make it four, so I go back outside, walk quickly past Coffee Messiah, jump in the air and start giggling. I go into Retrospect Records to look for Tina Turner, but they never have anything good. On my way back, I don't see the boy with green pants, so I figure he must be inside the cafe. I go up to my apartment again, but then I decide to eat my dolmas out on the front stoop and catch the guy as he walks back uphill.

Dean and Jake come out of the Hillcrest Market and I'm motioning with my finger, but they don't seem to notice or they don't recognize me because I shaved my head or something. Finally they come over, I say are you going home to drink, and I tell them about the boy with green pants. They say no we're going to Glo's, so I go with them. Nick's there, I kiss him and he says I've been at work for thirteen hours. He's waiting for a new dishwasher to be installed. He says I saw you walking home with your groceries and there was this boy watching you. I say did he have green pants? Nick says yes and I'm in hysterics, I tell him the story and Nick says well he was *definitely* following you, and then I rush down the hill.

I go into Coffee Messiah and sit down right next to the boy, I say I just heard that you were following me, so I had to come down here and talk to you. He looks kind of shocked, and actually he's not that cute, kind of straight-looking in a post-grunge sort of way. I say I thought it was funny when I saw you on Broadway and then down here, but my friend Nick who works at Glo's said you were definitely following me. He says I don't remember seeing you on Broadway—and he's holding hands with some woman who's probably his girlfriend. He has that blank look in his face like he doesn't know what *following* means, or where *Broadway* is, so I know he's lying. I introduce myself and then I run back up to Glo's.

Jake tells me about going to New York to hear Dean's band play and how they stayed with some woman in her thirty-fourth-floor penthouse, did coke with Phil Collins' son and Sean Lennon. Shook hands with Phil Collins but actually it was his twin brother. Snuck into Madonna's party after the MTV music awards and drank triple martinis and saw Puff Daddy and tipped the bartender ten dollars for each drink.

We decide to go to the Crescent, but first I run back up to my apartment to eat again, then I go down and meet them. They've all ordered this huge red drink called a Jesse Explosion, which is a wine cooler mixed with a mini-bottle of imitation champagne, over ice, in a thirty-two-ounce plastic cup. It's actually *tasty*—and only five dollars. This queen at the bar gives me a kiss and I smile but she looks insulted when I don't kiss her back. The mess at the table next to us puts a bra over his head like a bonnet, someone leans over and says is that what I *think* it is? We drink and Nick complains about the new cook at Glo's, some straightboy who tells stories about party chicks and insults all the old queers who come into the restaurant. I say why don't you just fire him—Nick's the manager or something because his sugar daddy or partner owns the place. Nick says he knows how to make eggs, I say just make the place vegan.

Jake starts blabbing about this boy who works at Pasta and Company, some muscleboy with lips like an octopus. Jake and Dean want to invite him over to their place and get him naked; they've got it all planned out—they're going to plug boiling pots of water into each of the eight outlets in their room, so then it'll get so steamy that Pasta Boy has to take off all his clothes. Jake and Dean will be wearing smoking jackets—and smoking, I guess—and then after Pasta Boy strips they'll get him to put a thong on his head and then Jake will have sex with him. I say why don't you have a threesome and Dean says *I'd* be into it. Nick and I exchange shady comments about *that* idea, Dean's one of those straightboys who's always talking about having sex with guys, but he never actually does anything. Just gets fags to fall for him: first Nick, then Andee, now I guess it's Jake's turn.

We decide to go to Sonya's, which is only five or ten blocks away, but Dean and Nick don't want to walk back up the hill so Nick drives, drunk. We stop at City Market so I can get something else to eat. Go to Sonya's and everyone gets cocktails but I get vermouth on the rocks. I'm not drinking cocktails any more because they make me want drugs. Besides, vermouth reminds Dean of the night I started drinking again after I stopped for seven months: there was that snowstorm and when the snow melted there was a foot of water pouring down the hill, two feet of slush on the sidewalk. Anyway at Sonya's they don't give me enough vermouth and Jake tells me he's going to move to New York in a few years and live in a three-thousand-dollar loft space. I say are you going to share it with ten people? He says no I'll live by myself because it'll be taken care of. I say honey no one lives by himself in a three-thousand-dollar loft space except for some *rich* person. He says well I'll make money *writing* and I just start laughing. I say what are you going to be writing? He says journalism, you can make that kind of money in journalism, and I'm wondering if Sean Lennon gave him that line. Then he's telling me there *are* poor people living in three-thousand-dollar loft spaces, they've just got the rent covered by their company.

Something's obviously wrong with Jake. I get a double vermouth and everyone else gets another cocktail and then we head up to this pool hall called the Break Room where Dean's meeting Sidney from his band. Nick goes home to flea bomb his house. I play pool with Dean, it's only my fourth time playing so I'm not quite a star. Solana shows up and I guess she's never hung out with me when I've been drinking beer, so she's kind of in shock. Dean starts blabbing about kissing his sweat towels with lipstick on, then throwing them into the audience at shows, says he wants to do whatever's tackiest and take it one step further. Solana and Sidney are enthralled or drunk and I'm bored. Solana and I play air hockey and then I leave.

I decide to stop by Neighbors for the first time in months, which is a mistake of course. It's '80s night which is a big hit in Seattle, one-dollar well drinks and usually cute boys. But no cute boys this week. I leave after ten minutes, think of going to Basic Plumbing because I might as well have sex. I'm taking off my bracelets so that I'll look more mainstream and this guy pulls up in his car, looks kind of cute so I look back at him. Then he pulls ahead of me, and I get in, what're you up to? Just hanging out.

He's grabbing his dick through his pants so I start grabbing my dick and pretty soon we're grabbing each other's dicks. He says do you want to go in the alley? He drives into the alley, which is brighter than the street, and we pull out our dicks. I start sucking on his neck and then biting and he starts moaning and I go down on him. I can't get the right angle to take his whole dick in my mouth comfortably so I'm worried that I'm hurting him. He pulls his dick out of my mouth and starts jerking off really fast like he's on speed, and I move towards him so he can grab my thigh while I jerk off. He says *nice* dick, I say you too. Catch myself looking to see if my dick's as big as his, I can't believe I'm still doing that.

Then he kisses me and he's still jerking really fast, like he's being shaken. He says lick my balls, but I don't really like licking balls so I lick them for a minute and then I go back to sucking his dick. I've got my hands on his chest and he starts to moan then takes his dick out of my mouth again and goes back to jerking off, I sit up and grab his balls while I squeeze the shaft of his dick. He's jerking faster than the speed of light or sound, I'm not sure which. He's panting and staring at my dick and shaking and then he comes, I want so badly to lick the come off his dick but I try to wait at least two minutes until it's probably safer. I only last about thirty seconds and then I slide my lips around his cockhead and down to the base. Tastes so fucking good.

Someone walks by and we pull up our pants, sort of, and then I take my dick out and spit on my hand and start stroking. I say grab my chest, and he grabs me, but not the right way. I say under my armpits and I turn towards him. He grabs me under my armpits and I get the surge I want, I say harder and he grabs me too hard. I say further back and then he's got my chest between his hands and I come, he says *yeah* shoot it, *yeah*, then I kiss him on the lips and he holds his tongue in my mouth.

I say do you have a napkin or something? He's got a towel—for wiping ashes off the dashboard. I wipe up and he says well I guess that's how faggots meet.

Andee's Endorphins

Andee just got a job at Microsoft, which is a sure path to success now that Bill Gates is Seattle's superstar: Kurt Cobain died and Courtney Love fled. Andee was never much of a Nirvana fan, but he did drive me up to Courtney's house once, this brick mansion with a twenty-foot-high wall around it. We stood in the park next door and a guard yelled GET AWAY. Andee's been in this town so long that he's already worked at Microsoft, this is his second time around. Last time it was his ticket to the big time, plaid Polo button-downs and a matching boyfriend named Andee. This time Microsoft is gonna be Andee's ticket away: he's gonna stop smoking pot so much, go to the Y and get some endorphins, get on a plane and get out of here.

Retin-A

In second grade, I always brought two bags of lunch to school: one for food and one for candy. People would talk to me to get the candy, but mostly I'd just crack one sour ball after another in my mouth until the chewing surfaces of my teeth were filled with bits of candy that I couldn't get out. At recess, I'd trade stickers with the girls: Scratch 'n' Sniffs, puffies, changees, and googley-eyes. My favorite stickers were the Hello Kittys and Holly Hobbys that my mother wouldn't let me buy — they were for girls. I wanted to get all of Holly Hobby's purses. I'd talk with the girls about how much we hated boys — they were so immature — while the boys waved sticks at us and called me sissy. Faggot. At home, there were faces in my blankets, monsters under the bed. I couldn't sleep in the dark.

The hostage crisis came and went. My sister, Lauren, and I sang "Thriller" in my grandmother Florence's Cadillac. Florence said my voice wasn't good, but Lauren might have talent. My grandmother Rose gave me a red nylon bag: you pulled out the inside of the bag and it turned into a jacket. Rose also gave us tiny, bright-colored plastic animals that you dropped in water and they turned into sponges. I'd hold the sponges over my crotch when my father would unlock the bathroom door with scissors to come in while I was showering.

At night, Lauren would scream HELP ME until my mother would soothe her back to sleep. I'd hold my breath. I dreamed of being smothered to death in shit, woke up screaming because there were eyes on my walls. In the morning, I'd chew my Flintstones vitamins and get a stomachache. One day

I looked at a picture of me as a baby and I figured I must have weighed more then than I did at ten. My father said most fat babies grow up to be fat adults, and I stopped eating. My sister and I watched Tina Turner in the "Private Dancer" video, my mother said can you believe she's forty? Tina had great legs, but her hair was a mess.

Besides Tina, Lauren and I liked Cyndi Lauper, and we thought Madonna was just some expensive copycat. Cyndi and Madonna were fighting it out on the charts and we were rooting for Cyndi. Cyndi had those gummi bracelets way before Madonna. Later, after Cyndi disappeared, I had a slumber party on my birthday, but I wasn't allowed to invite girls. We all went out to Ambrosia for dinner: Yohance, Kevin, Robert, Dennis and me. We leaned out the back window of my family's Datsun 510 hatchback (wasn't that neat?), and sang "Like a Virgin" to the passing cars. At home, we watched each other hump pillows on the floor like we were fucking. We called phone sex lines and talked about each others' peppermint sticks.

When I was studying, Lauren would scream for me. I'd run into the family room to find her pointing at some model on tv: She's so fucking beautiful—don't you want to *kill* her? Lauren got Benetton sweaters and I craved their softness. In sixth grade, the boys memorized the rap part of the Chaka Khan song "I Feel for You," and I thought Chaka Khan was the rapper. Lauren went to get a perm and I wanted one too, then my hair would stay in place and I wouldn't have to slick it back with mousse. I saw Lauren's perm and changed my mind.

On bad nights, Lauren would wave a knife at our parents and say I'm going to chop you up and put you in the frying pan. Lauren got acne before I did—even though she was two years younger. But then she got Retin-A, so she had one zit and I had two. I got Retin-A, which made me break out. Benji Goldberg gave me *Purple Rain* for my bar mitzvah, but the first tape I ever bought was Falco. In seventh grade, after I was in bed, I'd listen to the Top Ten at Ten on Q107 and "Rock Me Amadeus" stayed in the number one spot for a record number of weeks.

In sixth grade, I started paying attention to how I dressed, and in seventh grade all my girl friends started having crushes on the boys we used to hate together. I stopped talking to my father, except to argue; I practiced staring through his eyes until they were empty holes, and I could look out the window. For a while, I wore Generra t-shirts and wayfarer sunglasses with baggy pants, but soon I switched to black turtlenecks with mustard or army green v-neck sweaters, pegged black jeans and loafers. Jeannine Leflore saw me outside at recess one day and she said are you a mod? In art class, the trendies would play Madonna and the mods would play the Violent Femmes. I'd sit in the middle.

Jerome Stewart sang about not having to take your clothes off to have a good time, and I thought so, too. One day, after school, I was at the urinal in the bathroom at Woodie's department store and the man next to me got hard. I couldn't breathe. I reached over to touch it and he reached for mine. Someone came in and I zipped up my pants and ran. In ninth grade, I went to Woodie's almost every day. Always promising never again. My father and I argued about what refrigerator to buy, and I won.

Pulling Taffy

Since I had my prostate removed, Dave says, I can't get hard, but I can still have orgasms. I think I'm in touch with different nerves. When I come, I don't ejaculate and it feels almost like a female orgasm, from how I've heard it described. Now if you could just bend over me with your head that way, I could get a good look at your bottom.

We're at the Hot Tubs, in a tiny room lined with wood paneling from the '70s, metal siding to protect the walls, an alcove with a mattress squeezed into the corner. We're on the mattress. I try to watch my reflection in the siding as I bend over Dave, my ass in his face, fingers rubbing his balls. He puts his lips at my asshole and I get hard, thinking *eat my ass* like in a porn video. Thinking of another Dave, thirty years younger and a whole lot cuter. I was with him last night when I got paged. He said, do you want to call that trick, slid his lips around my dick, arms under my ass, and I moaned, held the back of his neck. Pulled his head off my dick and kissed him, tasting my own precome. I said I can't decide whether to come all over your chest or make that call.

This Dave says let me show you how to get me off — it's kind of like pulling taffy. You put a little lube on it and pull hard with one hand after the other. He demonstrates — we'll do that in a few minutes, first just pull on my cockhead like this. He's pulling gently on my cockhead with two fingertips. I'm standing over the bed, his hand underneath my ass, and I'm getting hard again even if I'd rather have a firmer touch, the other Dave on top of me. I picture last night, when he bit my neck while I held his head with one hand and my other hand slid down his pants to his asshole, he said this is a great way to be a bottom.

This Dave says yeah, now could you work on my cock, so I put some lube on my hand and start squeezing his dick, alternating hands. Feels more like milking a cow than pulling taffy. He says yeah, a little harder, and I'm squeezing really hard now, one hand then the other, closing my eyes and breathing in with each pull, out with each release. He says could you spread your legs a little...great, and I'm pulling on his dick, it's getting slightly longer. He has one hand on my dick and the other between my legs. I'm sweating because they've got the heat on 95 or maybe it's because of the sauna. I can feel the sweat rolling down the sides of my chest as I spit on my hand and keep pulling.

He says oh that feels great, could you squeeze a bit harder on my cockhead? It might seem like it's too hard, but believe me it feels good. Now I'm squeezing harder, pulling up and down, up and down, thinking I hope I get a tip for this. He says oh that's just right, I love that extra slide on my cockhead, so now I focus on the cockhead: squeeze and slide, squeeze and slide. He says that's great, it takes a few minutes — that feels just great. I open my eyes and look at him, hair rising off his chest, his face bright red, eyes half-open and fluttering. I think: what would happen if he died here? He wouldn't have enough money to make it worth my while to take his wallet and run, so I'd have to deal with the cops, they'd keep all the cash and then hold me for questioning.

I'm pulling on his cockhead, squeezing with one hand and then the other. He starts this high-pitched moan, sounds like he's gonna die but I know he's loving it. He says oh could you touch my balls a bit, not too much. I touch his balls and then move back to his cockhead, spit on my hand again and squeeze, slide. He's not touching me anymore, eyes closed, just squealing and moaning. I'm watching him like some strange creature — it's amazing and not quite funny, almost hot, and he grabs my hands, says just squeeze gently now. I hold his dick and squeeze the head. He sits up, says oh that was wonderful, just right. Do you think we could make it a once-a-week thing? When someone learns those techniques, I feel like it's an investment.

When the Night Ends

Male Hormonal Cycles

Today I wake up feeling like half of my head is missing. Andee says it's the full moon, I'm just sick of these fucking cycles. The only two times when I feel stable are when I'm working out and when I go to the beach. Otherwise it's Moodswing Nation: Andee, Robin and I are definitely heading up the Seattle chapter, though Andee and Robin aren't talking; I don't know how we're gonna process.

Sometimes I get these moments of calm, the longest was on the Fourth of July — believe it or not. When I was walking downtown. It was like my body's natural antidepressants just kicked in all the sudden, or maybe it was the Saint-John's-wort, but anyway I was smiling at all the tourists, felt like I was walking on air. But then it was back to sketched-out mess. Now I feel like I'm going to pull out my hair if I don't get outside. But I just shaved my head.

What I want to know is whether I'll ever have two good days in a row, whether I'll ever feel grounded on a regular basis, whether I'll ever be able to make any decisions between 10 and 12 at night. Mike from my survivors' group said maybe you were abused at that time. All the energy in my body went right to my head like I could breathe through my pores.

When the Night Ends

Sometimes it's hard to say when the night starts, but tonight definitely starts when they play "Block Rockin' Beats" at the Eagle. "Block Rockin' Beats" is the Chemical Brothers song that you hear in every club now — from house to jungle to trance. And apparently even at the Eagle, where the music usually ranges from Heart to Poison. Brandon says it was inevitable, but I'm not sure this isn't his first time at the Eagle. Anyway they play "Block Rockin' Beats" and I'm feeling it, ready for that hard house trance night at the Eagle and then they go right into Pink Floyd.

Mike and Brandon are a strange couple. Mike's kind of a mainstream muscleboy and Brandon's this raver transitioning into clubkid. Brandon's getting into makeup and Mike certainly seems like he loves it. The two of them are such a rare sight, all the sudden I'm wanting a butch boyfriend too. Then I won't have to worry about pulling off masculine realness to be an item at the bar.

For a few minutes I want to be high so badly I can't speak. Luckily I'm in Seattle, where no one sticks their keys up to my nose. But sometimes the craving lasts for hours. I mean I haven't done drugs for over a year, except for bad acid twice when I was too drunk, but what it comes down to is that I still haven't learned to live *without* drugs.

Cookie Mueller says to make sure you're never lonely, fill your day with lots of activities, but anyway tonight my craving doesn't go away. I go to City Market with Andee to buy herbal energy pills, I'm gonna cut them up and snort them. Get home and Andee's waiting for me to go to Basic Plumbing, I'm sketching out about whether I want to go. I have this big silent drama about the herbal energy pills, think either I'm gonna stay with myself or I'm going to do drugs — or fake drugs, anyway. I throw the pills out the window and it feels good, though why does everything have to be such a fucking battle?

I go to Basic Plumbing with Andee, even though all I really want to do is dance. Pretty soon I'm jerking this guy off and he starts kissing me like crazy then comes all over my legs, smiles and says I don't usually kiss. Then this other guy comes into the backroom, he's young and slim and I get right on my knees to suck his cock while I run my hands up and down his chest. I suck for two or three thrusts and then he pulls his dick away though I'd definitely take his come, he's the only guy here I'm really attracted to. He starts jerking off really fast, shoots on the floor, zips up his pants and runs away.

The funny thing about Basic Plumbing is that since it's the center of my sexual life, I manage to find moments of intimacy. After the cute guy runs away, I stand up and say *he didn't even say thanks* and the other guys in the room kind of chuckle, then I'm sucking some other guy's dick, taking it all in my throat. The guy next to him keeps saying wow, he's really good, he's got some talent. Probably wants me to move over to his dick but the other guy's dick is what I want, big and thick and almost choking me. At one point I choke hard, say *that's what I get from smoking too much* and we all start laughing, Andee tells me later that he heard me from the other room. The guy whose dick I'm sucking asks if I want to get some privacy but I don't, I kiss him and say I think I'm gonna walk around. The other guy says you're a lot of fun, kisses me and then we hug.

I look for Andee to say goodbye but he's disappeared; he can hear me but I don't know that yet so I don't say anything. There's no one around who I want to play with, so I leave. On my way home, this guy says are you available? He isn't too cute so I say no I'm heading home, he says you've got a great ass, could you bend over to tie your shoe? Funny how sexual compliments come in streaks for me: two guys had a conversation about my ass in the backroom earlier at Basic Plumbing. So I bend over slowly to tie my shoe and then keep walking.

Of course Gary O'Henry pulls up in his Jaguar, I played with him one night on my way home from Basic Plumbing and lost one of my earrings in his car. I step in to get my earring, there's Gary O'Henry with his huge dick, but I'm not in the mood. I know he'll pay me if I let him fuck me, but he'd have to give me a whole bottle of poppers to take that thing.

Inside Me

I grew up worrying that I'd get AIDS from tasting my own come. Whenever I finished masturbating, I'd play with the puddle in front of me, studying its texture and its warmth. The smell of my come would get me high, but when I finally dared to lick some off my fingers, it tasted like plastic. Afterwards, I washed my mouth out with Listerine — my father's Listerine — even though I hated Listerine and I hated my father.

Dan says I wanna be inside you. He's holding my legs over his shoulders, pressing his dick against my asshole, and I let him. In. He says I promise I won't come inside you. I try to sound seductive: why don't you just put on a condom and then you can come whenever you want to. He starts whining. Tyler, I love being inside you.

I've had a few drinks — and Dan is my thousand-dollar trick — so I don't get too annoyed. I let him fuck me without a condom, I even relax enough to get hard again. I say do you want me to come? He says yes and he's jerking my dick, grabbing my armpits just the way I asked him to. But I've already come once, it's his turn so I can rest. I say and then you're going to jerk off on my chest? He says Tyler, I wanna come inside you. I want to tell him how cheesy that line is. I say I just let you fuck me for another half hour, and I'm sick of the struggle so I sit all the way down on his dick, pull his hands back to my armpits. He moans.

I'm getting fucked in a beachfront condo on the carpet by the fireplace. By the fireplace that reminds me of the basement where my father held me over the sink, covered my mouth, and slid his dick into my ass. But that's not what I want to think about. I try to stay aroused. I think about what I should do if Dan comes inside me. I'll have to throw a fit, say now you owe me at least fifteen hundred. An extra five hundred. It doesn't sound that bad.

Dan doesn't come inside me. He falls into a drunken sleep a few minutes after we move to the bed. I take a shower, do yoga, write in my journal, and try to get tired enough to sleep with him. As I'm about to pass out on the floor, I get up and lie down next to him.

I wake up with his dick pressing between my legs, poking at my asshole, his hand reaching around me to grab my dick. I want to scream. I pull his hand off my dick and rest it on my thigh, move my ass away from him. He's holding me and I'm trying to relax, trying to fall back asleep, but all I can think about is taking a sledgehammer and knocking off his head. We're in the basement of my father's house, I take a sledgehammer and knock off his head. Whoops! No blood because then it gets too messy.

Metronome

You say sometimes my brain feels like a golf ball swinging back and forth inside my head and it makes me dizzy. I can't stand up. And sometimes it's like a fish in a fishbowl that's so small the fish has to bend in half. I can't swim.

After Sewing Class

I'm getting all crazy because I haven't eaten in a few hours, walking as fast as I can so I'll get home before I fall apart. I pass this park and some skinheads are hanging out or maybe they're fags with white shirts and suspenders. I hear them whistling at me as I walk past, but actually I can't tell if it's them whistling. Then they're making this chicken noise so I turn around and blow them a kiss. Someone says ooh I want more, and it's a queeny voice, or maybe it's a straightboy imitating a queen.

I keep walking, but then I think wait a second, were they flirting with me? Did I miss out on something? Or were they calling me chicken? I mean, I think they were young too but I didn't really look. James told me I looked like chicken when I saw him just after I shaved my head. Maybe they were gay skins. Or maybe it was Andee, he's been all into skinheads lately.

I get home and eat, then I have twenty minutes before 9:30 when I'm supposed to meet Steve at the Eagle. I clean the dishes and try to organize my room. 9:30 and I'm on my way out the door when I decide that I have to change my pants, just can't stand the pants I'm wearing anymore because they're too loose at the ass. So I change my pants, run out the door at 9:35. Stop at City Market to get a Rice Dream Moon Pie, rush to the Eagle.

Steve's at the pay phone, I say I'm not that late am I? He says they're playing Bruce Springsteen. We start walking and I start blabbing but where are we going? I want to sit outside, so we end up back at the Eagle. They're not playing Springsteen anymore. Steve shows me a picture of the serial killer he used to know. The serial killer reminds me of this boy Robbie from Boston. We called him Champagne. He was this queen from the suburbs who talked about all his drag outfits — Armani, Versace, Gaultier — but no one ever saw him in drag. He just walked around saying don't make me *read* you miss one. Talked about all his money, but then he took the locks off our doors with a screwdriver to steal drugs and money and Calvin Klein underwear when we were out.

The serial killer's wearing a Nautica jacket and he's got Champagne's smile. Steve's telling me the story and I'm watching this boy who looks cute but I can't really tell because it's too dark. I go to the bathroom, come back and Steve's ready to leave. He's walking towards me so I can't see the boy to say goodbye — or *let's fuck later* — and I can sense from his friends that they were waiting for something.

I leave with Steve and now I'm obsessing about the boy I haven't met *and* the skinheads in the park. Steve's amusing me though; he's good at telling stories. We go to Rosebud and he reads me some of the press about the serial killer. Then this boy who I had sex with in the Convention Center bathroom walks by, I say honey I see you *everywhere*. He's with some other straightboy and he has this shocked confused look on his face, keeps on walking. So then I tell Steve that story.

Interview

Interview

When I see Ed Koch across the street from me, I don't recognize him. But then the man who's selling me sandals says *look*. People's Court Ed makes quite the spectacle, waving at each person who says hey. Everyone seems to know it's him — except me, a new New Yorker.

Now, some of you might argue that this is Ed Koch's territory, right in front of the building he shares with Larry Kramer and who knows how many other megalomaniacal, dogmatic, reactionary, rabid hypocritical assholes. Ed Koch is nobody's West Coast whore. I mean East Coast-transported-to-West Coast hooker. I mean East Coast-fled-to-West Coast-back-to-East Coast-no-West Coast-now-on-the-East Coast-dreaming-of-West Coast ho.

I'm the callboy giving airs to Ed Koch for looking at me across the street after I've been staring at him, trying to figure him out. Because Eddie looks dazed. I'm talking sky-high, floating above the clouds, no now you can't even see the clouds: way-out confused and disoriented. Except then Ed's looking at me like he's trying to place me, but then I realize no he's giving me *that* look, the one my tricks give me.

Now I'm not trying to say that all my tricks give me the same look, book, cook — no, listen, I'm not trying to say that all my tricks give me full Ed Koch. I'm just saying that when I had dinner with this writer who told me one story after the other about his decadent and glamorous '70s, I didn't think of Ed Koch, even though the apparently decadent and glamorous but not yet seventy-year-old writer *did* look at me. I looked back.

But mostly it was that writer who looked back: at everything from Katherine Hepburn's late-night adventures with Farrah Fawcett in the Mineshaft trough room, to the time Bette Midler got caught by the paparazzi while fist-fucking Warren Beatty at the Black Party. But weeks after I see Ed Koch fisting Larry Kramer at the Black Party — I mean on Eighth Street — no wait, I'm buying sandals, right: sandals.

Here's where the sandals end and the story begins. Two British guys call me, one after the other; they're friends and they want to see me back-to-back. They've got me confused, but only a little. I head over to see the first trick — his name's Nick, and we're meeting at his office in Soho. The security guard lets me in, he calls Nick Kevin, which is no surprise; at least he didn't call himself John. Let's call him Dick.

The office is enormous and posh: huge bookcases, dividers made of mahogany instead of that weird soundproof carpet stuff. Dick can't find the lights, we're wandering around to figure out where he wants to have sex. I say what kind of office is this? He says it's sort of a magazine.

I go to the bathroom, and when I get out something looks different, I'm not sure what. Did I walk out the right way? I call Nick, Dick, I even try Rick, Vic, Brick, Stick... Then I try Sick, but I realize his name's Kevin, right, Kevin. No answer and the lights are all off except by the bathroom, which is also by the elevator. Now I realize what's changed: Dick opened the doors on both sides, right?

I'm kind of freaked out, so I go back into the bathroom. Maybe I need to fix my hair. But no, only one exit. Kevin's gone and I can't find any lights. I don't really want to walk into the dark; I'd just leave but my backpack's gone. I've got at least five hundred dollars in there and all my identification, not to mention dinner and my gym shoes. I've only got three dollars in my pocket, that's not even enough for a cocktail.

I'm yelling for Kevin; finally I find some lights, but they're on the opposite side from where we went. It's this huge room full of computers and *Interview* folders, guess that's where I am. Sort of a magazine. I'm thinking Kevin probably wouldn't want to slash my head off with a machete right in the *Interview* office, blood all over the carpet, but then it's probably stainproof, right? And it would make a great cover: four shots of my head in different colors.

Then I find the actual Warhols—it's a room full of them, but that's as far as I can get. I hear motion sensors going off whenever I move around, but no sign of Kevin. I go back to the other side but still no lights; I wouldn't mind wandering through *Interview* if there were just some fucking lights. Though every now and then I hear tiny noises in the room like papers shuffling, footsteps, twigs snapping. Wait a second... I turn around and yell AM I AN EXTRA IN *THE BLAIR WITCH PROJECT*?

I don't know what to do. Luckily I've got my cellphone, not just for a brain tumor but to call my roommate Jon when my trick turns into an *Interview* stalker. I tell Jon the story and now I'm wired, he's confused and I'm pacing. Is this the same entrance? I decide to go downstairs and see what the guard can tell me. I get on the elevator, and the doors shut, but none of the floors will light up. Jon's on the phone with me and he sounds freaked out, so I decide to stay calm.

Luckily the elevator opens up again—no

machine gun, but what the fuck? I push "S" and that lights up, maybe that's the lobby. I get to "S" but no it's the basement, Jon's saying wait so he has your bag, yes he has my bag. I don't really want to get off in the basement, there's a door straight ahead but what if it's locked? I'm getting all paranoid and so's Jon, there are red lights flashing outside and what if that's the cops? What if I've been set up and Kevin's stolen something? More headlines: Male Prostitute Nabbed with Warhol's Mao.

I push all the buttons on the elevator, but nothing works. Finally I notice an intercom, I say I need to get out in the lobby. All the sudden five lights up. The guard's voice comes through, he says you can't get out in the lobby. Jon and I both agree that something's up with that. I tell the guard there's no way I'm going back up to five, but he's telling me to stop blocking the doors. I don't know what to do. Jon doesn't know either.

I decide to go for the outside world, push open the doors — yes, they're unlocked — I'm outside, there are no sirens just tourists. I go back to the front, into the lobby and there's the guard. He's got rings under his eyes like football makeup and he's totally belligerent, kind of yelling at me; Jon and I are both thinking what the fuck? I decide to play some tough-guy act, telling Jon the address over and over again like he's my pimp and there's gonna be trouble. You know: trouble.

The guard tells me I shouldn't go into buildings when I don't know what's going on, but I'm not looking for cautionary tales that aren't my own. I tell him I went upstairs and Kevin disappeared with my bag. I'm not leaving until I get my bag. Finally the guard agrees to call Kevin but Kevin doesn't answer. I'm talking to Jon—what should I do? I'm pacing in the lobby, looking at the antique vacuum cleaners in a glass case—that's the decoration.

All I can think about is cocktails, food, cocktails, food, cocktails, food, cocktails. Then it becomes clearer: steamed vegetables with rice at Dojo, Stoli Vanilla on the rocks with extra lemon, Stoli Vanilla on the rocks with extra lemon. I wasn't gonna drink anymore because then I always end up in some messy coke den, but fuck that shit, I'm so edgy I feel like I'll explode if I don't get some alcohol into my body—fast.

Now, I can do lots of things at once, for example: talking on the phone with Jon/my pimp, I'm arguing with the doorman/guard (or does he even work here?), pacing back and forth, looking at the vacuum cleaners, thinking about cocktails... Food First: an aid agency for times like these. And the guard's talking to Kevin—Kevin's sending my bag down—there's my bag but no Kevin. Jon says look inside, I look inside—everything's there and so I'm no longer—*taxi*.

They almost won't let me order at Dojo because it's too late or something, I page Rina and she's leaving the Clit Club so we agree to meet at the Phoenix in twenty minutes. The food's fine, but I don't know what they gave me as a cocktail; I send it back. Run out of that place—GET ME TO A BAR— plus I'm late, damn it, but I get to the Phoenix and Rina's not there yet, or at least she's not outside.

I go into the bar, and there's a doorman, what's that about? He cards me and I throw him shade, he says well you look like you're twelve. I say exactly—and twelve-year-olds should be able to drink in the East Village. I pull out my license anyway, ask him if he's seen Rina, well he doesn't know Rina but has he seen any women at all waiting around? No.

I part the crowd for the bar; they don't have Stoli Vanilla, but they do have Stoli, so I'm okay. There's Whitney and the boy whose name I can't remember, damn—have they seen Rina? No. I go downstairs to the bathroom, back upstairs and outside—no Rina. Back to the bar for another cocktail and then I tell Whitney and the boy my story, it's the boy who I originally met, but for some reason it's Whitney's name I remember. Rina thinks Whitney's hot—and she is—so if Rina were here we could all be flirting. Anyway I tell the two my story and they're scandalized but intrigued and actually kind of worried for me too; they go to the Wonder Bar and I get another cocktail.

Pretty soon I'm smashed and Rina hasn't arrived, I've got a group around me at the bar. I spot Gary and he tells me about Joe who's hot but he has a boyfriend, then there's Russ who's so drunk he's drooling and swaying on his stool, plus some guy in a suit who's trying to act all classy. Then there's Nicky Z, it's all about me and Nicky Z—I always find the eighteen-year-old party girl. Plus her friend.

Then the bar's closing—what?—and even though I've assured myself over and over again that I'm drunk but luckily I'm not craving coke, I head over to the afterhours coke bar with Nicky Z, her friend, and even Russ and his friend. We're going to the one with dancing—on Avenue B—but when we get there they're playing reggae and there's no coke to be found.

I kiss my goodbyes and run to Green's—there

may not be any dancing but there sure as hell will be coke. I walk right in and there's Dante, can I get a bag? There's my bag and then I go right over to the bar and dump about half of it on the backside of an ashtray. That's the best thing about Green's — you can do your coke on the bar, even though most people hide in the corner or the bathroom anyway. Everybody's scared or greedy.

I do a line and then I ask the woman next to me if she wants some, sure, and then I look over and no way there's Jayne County. I've never met her but I've read her autobiography, *Man Enough to Be a Woman*, so I say hey Jayne. She says oh hi, I say you want a line? She says oh, thanks. Does her line and then says where do I know you from? I say oh you know — around. I go to the bathroom because the laxative in the coke is hitting.

Then I'm feeling much better, the coke's what I needed, everything's wonderful right now — I should just leave and go home. But then Jayne takes out her coke and we've got a trio now — me, Jayne, and the snotty uncomfortable woman in between us — Diane. I guess Diane came with Jane but I can't imagine how they're friends. Jayne starts talking about how isn't this the best place in the world — it's all that's left, it's real, it's what New York should be. I'm thinking I hate this place and we're doing more coke and then I'm way too wired of course; I order cocktails and get two more bags and then I'm on the toilet again.

Back at the bar, Jayne's talking about how she just loves the trade at Green's, how she wants to get a piece of cock but I just want pot, honey, pot. No one's got any; of course Diane never touches the stuff. I go into the other room and there's this whole group of Eurotrash, I offer them coke for pot but no luck. I go up to literally everyone. There's one fun woman who I give a bump to anyway, then one of the Eurotrash hands me a joint. I say thank you so much, he says I just want you to shut up.

I go back to Jayne and Diane, with the new woman—Katie—and we all do a line. I smoke the whole joint 'cause no one else wants any, and anyway, I want the whole joint. It kind of calms me. Jayne's saying there was Berlin in the '30s, London in the '60s, and New York in the '70s, right? She says that's the truth, right? I say sure.

Jayne tells me everyone thinks she's Lady Bunny, if one more person says that she's gonna smack them. At this point we're all basically shaking 'cause the coke's gone on and on, Jayne's out of money and I've already bought five bags—no more to share. So we head outside, whoops it's bright. I hug Jayne goodbye and then I walk over to the peepshow on Fourteenth.

7 a.m. and no one's there, I do more coke in one of the booths—I've got some left from each bag. Then I'm staring at the porn and wow I'm so turned on. Coke's not really sexual for me until I'm kind of crashing, but the porn is definitely doing it. I figure if I can get hard I'll walk through the cold to the West Side Club—7 a.m. on a Saturday it's jumping. Sure enough I get hard, watching the guy on the screen just pound the other guy's ass—I wanna be pounded I wanna pound, I want come all over my face I want to smell that dirty drugged-out sex smell.

I zip up my pants and practically run to the West Side Club, take off my earrings and bracelets outside, and then I'm inside, clothes off and in a towel, into a bathroom stall for a bump. The place is packed, lots of hot boys who are flying or crashing or both. It actually scares me how packed it is — all the drugs — but tonight I'm a part of it and I'm ready.

I walk right into a room with these two dreamy guys — I've never used that word before but here it fits 'cause that's what they were. I mean the people who would describe them would say dreamy, meaning Chelsea clones with an all-American sensibility, a masculinity that appears authentic enough to wear Prada Sport without exposing any limp wrists. But here of course they're wearing nothing, I'm wearing Prada Sport. No I'm wearing nothing — I wouldn't be caught dead in Prada Sport — but *gross* am I passing as a Chelsea clone?

Okay, maybe I'm passing as a Chelsea clone with fucked-up hair — or in any case I'm in that dreamy den within seconds. One guy's sucking my cock and the other one's jerking his dick — I love his grin and I need his dick in my mouth, it's thick and almost diagonal when it sticks out. Then the other guy leans against the wall and the guy with the diagonal dick is pounding him, and he's sucking my dick.

Sure I knew I was walking into barebacking central, sure it turns me on and shakes me beyond belief, makes me shake or is that the coke? It's my dick, I'm shaking, this guy's opening his asshole further and getting pounded and the guy with the grin is grinning and I'm grinning too and then the guy getting fucked pulls my dick into his asshole and I'm doing the pounding, plus I've got that diagonal dick in my mouth.

It's the absolute objectification that freaks me out and turns me on, but worse than that it's killing us, right? I told myself I wouldn't fuck anyone without a condom because of all the times someone's just shoved it into me without asking. I wanted to take responsibility for everyone's safety because no one's taking responsibility for mine.

The guy I'm fucking is cooing porn talk and the other guy — he's the dreamy one for me — just climbs on top of me and his dick is in my ass and I'm still fucking the other guy and you know this is my number one fantasy that's never quite happened, not the unsafe part but the double stuff. My ass feels chafed, which means this is extra-unsafe, my ass is burning but wow I'm getting fucked while I'm fucking, I know I'm fucked but fuck!

It's amazing, the whole chain of sensation: my body's in between these two bodies and connected to both and we're all moaning and sweating and pounding. If we were wearing condoms this wouldn't be happening — someone would be struggling to stay hard or get hard or get fucked. Of course I'm thinking the guy fucking me could come in my ass and this would all change, nothing would change and we'd all be changed. What if I couldn't cry, but now the guy who's fucking me is hurting me too much, I lean forward his dick slides out and he shoves it back in. I love that. It hurts and I should never let it happen but I love the way he's grabbing my hips, the look on his face that I can feel even though I can't see it: this asshole's mine.

But wait this asshole's me. I pull out and away; I'm sucking the guy's dick and then he's worn out, needs a break and I grab them both and kiss them and I'm out in the hall, back to my locker, to the bathroom for a bump, into the hallway. I know I should have gotten off with those two guys because nothing will be as good, but this club's all about more,

more, more.

I'm walking in the hallway, around and around because there's no sex allowed outside of rooms — you might get kicked out and sent to do time on Mayor Giuliani's clean streets. I go into a room with this guy — I'm kissing him, he's sucking my dick, I'm sucking his dick; I say do you want me to fuck you and he does and then I slide it in without a condom and it feels amazing.

I'm kissing him and fucking him nice and slow and I say I won't come inside you, but why should he trust me? The one time I did come inside someone I felt like the most disgusting person on the face of the earth. Even though the guy begged me for it, held my dick in his ass. Even though I'm negative. That's when I vowed not to fuck without condoms.

But then there's this guy I'm fucking without a condom, long and hard and soft and fast, slow, in, out, in circles. I'm kissing and grabbing him and I'm grunting 'cause fuck it's hot, I'm hot and sweaty I can smell the drugs and the guy and I'm aching, groaning and all serious and anxious with come and some strange masculinity I'm only beginning to understand. I say do you want to come. He nods, I take my dick out of his ass and we're both jerking off furiously, he shoots his come onto my dick and I use it to keep jerking — there was a time when even that would have felt unsafe, but that time's past — I'm groaning and moaning, my body's all tense, deep breath and then I shoot all over him. I love it when I shoot, the best orgasm is painful right until it explodes — I explode and then collapse on top of him.

I kiss him and then we introduce ourselves, that was hot, I go into the shower. I smell like everybody else's sweat — rotten — which is great but

I wash it off anyway. Cute guys in the shower cruising me, but I've gotta go. Dressed and then out into the cold, bright sun which is kind of nice because I've barely seen the sun since my Seasonal Affective Disorder kicked in. I buy some chips but I can't eat them, over to Union Square to stare at the sun but then I get into a cab, head home, throw off my clothes, take some pills, get in bed.

There's always the next day, sometimes that's good and sometimes it's not. The next day it's not so good. Can't decide who to call, what to wear, how I'm gonna get out of the house. I've got coke left but I'm not gonna do it, though I can't bring myself to throw it away: there's kind of a lot. I get out of the house and it's dark but wow it's *warm*, everything's fine until I get to the subway, waiting and edgy. But then the ride on the subway's fine, I'm fine, it's gonna be fine. But where am I going?

I go to Black-Eyed Suzie's for dinner because they give you bread and dip so I don't go crazy while I'm waiting. The dip's better than ever and the food's okay, I flirt with the boy who always flirts with me and every other fag in the restaurant. Check my messages and there's Rina saying where were you, so I call her. Says she was at the Phoenix, waited forty-five minutes and where was I? She and Susan were worried about me, am I okay?

I'm okay, but I don't understand what happened. Then I get a call and it's some sketcher, coked out of his mind and do I like to party? Usually I'd say no, but today I say sure, he says what do you like? I say ecstasy, he says I'll get you ecstasy. But then he's gotta figure something out, he'll call me back.

I'm edgy, walking around the East Village

because it's so warm. I go to Stuyvesant Park but it's too early for cruising — just dog-walkers. Then the guy calls back, how soon can you get here? A half hour. He wants me to hurry, but first I've gotta go to a bar and change my pants. Tricks can't deal with green pants. I go to the Phoenix, which is crowded. Then jump into a cab and I'm off to Fifth Avenue.

Get to the trick's place and it's posh, one of those huge modern buildings with two doormen and a receptionist. Head upstairs and he opens the door in a robe, come with me. We head to the bathroom and he says here's two hundred — always a good sign when they pay you first. Then we go to the living room, which is a drug den for sure — three naked guys struggling to get hard on the puffy sofa, a pile of coke on the table.

These guys are washed out and I assume they're whores too but I don't know. They're all big but not quite buff, in their mid-thirties I guess. One of them's got this huge dick and a funny smile, keeps grabbing his dick and shoving it against the trick's asshole, which isn't what the trick wants. The trick pushes the coke over to me and hands me a rolled-up twenty, I say can I get something to drink. He says what do you want, love? Stoli on the rocks.

The trick comes back with my drink and I swallow about half of it — love the heat in my head. The trick's jerking off furiously and I can tell he's never gonna get hard, which is a relief because he told me he wanted to fuck me. Apparently he hasn't forgotten about the coke, though — I don't want to do any, but he pushes it towards me and I do a line: not this again.

Then one of the guys grabs my head and I'm sucking his dick so I get hard too, even though it's *freezing* in the apartment—the trick says he likes it cold because he's got bad sinuses. Wonder why. Then he takes out a blue pill and hands it to me, I swallow it down with a sip of vodka and then the coke's in my face again—no thanks, it messes with the e. But then I do another line anyway.

The trick's trying to get this blond boy to do the e, he's not much of a boy, but I can tell that's what he's supposed to be. Apparently the blond boy has to get up in the morning. The trick says what do you have to do, the boy says go to the gym and the trick's not having it, keeps handing the pill to the boy and the boy keeps putting it on the table. Finally I take the pill and swallow it, the trick says we know what you like and I smile; I'm such a drug fiend even when I don't want drugs.

The trick comes over to me and I'm sucking his dick, he's rubbing my chest and I'm thinking when is this over, when is the e gonna kick in? The other guys are kind of playing around but no one's really connecting—too much coke, plus I don't know if anyone understands what's going on; I don't. The trick's looking me in the eyes and I know how to look back, like I'm feeling it, he does more coke and then he pulls me by the hand and guides me into the bedroom.

We're in bed and everything's comfy, he says wait here sweetheart I want you for myself. So I wait while he goes into the other room. I think I hear money and shuffling feet but who knows. Everything in the room is beige except the lacquered brown walls and the white bed. That "floating about the clouds" song comes on and I almost laugh. I'm not high yet but I'm relaxed.

The trick comes back in with our drinks and

a pile of coke, he says how's my baby? I say I'm great. He gets in and we're making out, he tastes like an infinite number of cigarettes but he's a good kisser so I get into it. He's on top of me, grinding his dick against me and I'm hard, then I see the door open and there's one of the guys from the other room, jerking off. I wouldn't mind him joining us 'cause he's cute enough and he's got a nice dick, plus I think he might be another trick. But the main trick gets up and motions him out, says I'll be right back, okay? Do you need anything? Just water.

I lay back and in a few minutes the trick comes back with a bottle of Evian and more coke, which he just picks up between his fingers and snorts. His eyes are bulging and he's kissing me again, I put his hands on my chest and he's rubbing me, saying oh baby, oh baby. Then he turns me over and he's on top of me, I guess the ecstasy's kicking in because I sort of don't know where I am. The trick's on top of me and he feels nice and warm.

The trick moves over, lies back and pulls my head to his crotch so I start sucking his dick. I'm sucking and sucking and his dick is slowly getting harder, kind of like magic I think but not quite. When he's sort of hard, he pulls away and reaches for more coke, then a condom. I know he's never gonna be able to fuck me, but I figure I'll humor him. I lay on my back and he gets on top of me, squeezing his dick in his fist and trying to shove it in my asshole.

I'm looking the trick right in the eyes and he's got the I-love-you-but-I'm-wired, ecstasy-plus-cocaine look, I've got the this-is-so-meaningful, ecstasy-plus-work look. The trick realizes he's not gonna be able to fuck me this way, so he flips me over, starts pounding the outside of my ass with his limp dick. I say I'm gonna piss and get some water.

I go into the bathroom and the "floating above the clouds" song is playing again or maybe it's been playing all along or maybe this is a different song. I look in the mirror and yep my pupils are huge. I'm feeling that here-we-go-again ecstasy flip-flop, like I'm high but since there's no such thing as good ecstasy any more, I'm not gonna get *there*. I'm concentrating to piss while I look at the photo of a dripping muscleboy over the toilet, guess that's there to help me.

I piss, get some water from the kitchen and then head back to the bedroom. Luckily the trick's taken off the condom, which means he's given up on fucking me. He's jerking his dick and he says hi sweetheart like we've been lovers forever but he loves me more every time he sees me. He takes a sip of my water and I sit on his lap, facing away. He holds me and it feels good, we're both breathing a lot and feeling the ecstasy. He lights a cigarette and I turn toward him to suck on his nipples like a baby, lick his chest, his inner thighs.

Then I'm sucking his cock and I reach up to grab his nipples. He starts moaning and I think good the nipples are the key. His dick starts to get harder and he pulls my head up to make out. Then he pushes my head away and says wow, no one's grabbed my tits like that since Randy, he died of cancer last year. I can't believe people still say cancer, the look in the trick's eyes is thankful but mourning. I grab his tits and he starts jerking off, I say come all over my chest because I want to get this over with but also because I like getting come on my chest.

The trick sits over me, luckily he's not paying attention to my dick because I'm never gonna get hard. I'm grabbing his nipples and he's moaning and I'm going right into his eyes and actually it almost does feel like we're lovers: there's safety in this comfortable bed with expensive sheets and all the drugs I want, maybe stay at home and cook, call people on the phone, do more drugs.

I'm thinking this is my ticket to the big time, which is ridiculous because it never is, I'm high, I didn't used to think this way but however-many years as a whore changes you. The trick's still jerking off and I'm grabbing his tits and massaging his chest and this goes on for hours I swear, maybe even days or years — the ball drops, the third millennium passes and we're still in the same position, I'm getting arthritis. He's on top of me gritting his teeth and I'm underneath him chewing on my tongue and all four of our eyes are wide. I keep moving his extra hand from the bed to my chest because I like the feeling of all his weight balanced on me. All of his weight is balanced on me and I'm pulling harder on his tits, our eyes are together but we're both up somewhere, up, up.

But also I'm down, down, he's jerk jerk jerking, more lube, I spit, his hand's back on the bed, back on my chest, I can feel something nice in my groin though I don't know what. He's still jerking, I'm grabbing his tits with spit, he's moaning, he's looking me in the eyes, his hand's back on the bed, back on my chest — I have to get up, I'm gonna get up in a second okay if this goes on for another minute — and then his whole body goes tense and there it is, his come dripping onto my chest and he pulls away to light a cigarette.

I just lie there but pretty soon I have to piss, so I sit up to kiss the trick on the cheek and go into the bathroom. There's the guy with water dripping off his hair and the music gets much louder, I go back into the bedroom and say let's take a shower. The trick looks confused and happy, he says a shower?

Yeah, a shower — it'll feel nice — and then we're in the shower. Black granite walls and lots and lots of pressure, spacious, warm water. He's soaping me up and I'm thinking that showers are one of the best things about tricks — showers and towels. Showers where the tiles go to the ceiling, the water pressure is strong, the towel a vacation — not like that freezing-cold, mold-covered thing at my house. The trick's soaping me up with warm warm water. His turn: I'm soaping him up and there's the cloud song again, I almost believe it.

We get out of the shower and he's drying me off, feels safe and snug and he's kissing my neck. I'm thinking about the big time again: the apartment he's gonna get me, the trips to Europe. I say let's go to the store for a snack. He says you want to go outside? I say it'll be great. He says all right, honey.

I ask if I can borrow some clothes. He says anything you want honey, and we look each other in the eyes; these are the e moments. He takes out a huge pair of starched designer jeans, plus a baggy sweater and a puffy coat; I'm wondering if these are his clothes or his dead lover's. Then we head into the hall, hand in hand — we get into the elevator, I look like someone else and so does he. Downstairs, we pass all the doorpeople, out into the air, yes the air yes.

The air's great, 6 a.m. and it's still dark but look at all the lights in the shops. I say we should stop at the bank so you can pay me for the night, good thinking. But the bank will only let him take out forty extra dollars tonight—oh well. I look him in the eyes and say I can trust you for it, right? He says you can trust me; we'll see. We get to the store and I lose myself in the aisles—peppermint tea, red zinger, St-John's-wort berry juice, lemons, pumpernickel bread. I bring it all to the counter and that juice is wonderful, I'm waiting for the Vitamin C rush and we're back on the street, it's cold but fresh, the trick keeps repeating I can't believe we're out here, I say but it's great right it's great?

We get back upstairs and I think it's over for the trick, he says do you want to go to sleep? I say do you have any sleeping pills. We each take one and I go to make tea, can't decide whether I like the peppermint better or the berry. I'm staring at the colors, sniffing the liquids and the trick comes in from another world, he says let's get in bed. Bed—right—I'm still wired but I've learned my lesson—the drugs aren't gonna get any better so I might as well try to sleep. The trick starts to snore and I'm up gritting my teeth. Finally I get out of bed and go to my bag for a melatonin; there's an extra eighty dollars on the table that I think the other guy left for me, I put it in my bag. Now the trick just owes me another five hundred.

I take a melatonin and get in bed, something loud is going on in the park—a concert? Sounds like thousands of people and the room reeks of smoke and the trick's snoring. Finally I doze off but not really. At some point the trick gets up and much later I get up too. He's smoking in the living room and smiling at my naked body; I'm a wreck. A shower wakes me up, what was all that noise? The marathon, honey—oh, what time is it?—5 p.m. I better get home, though I'm not sure why.

I think of wearing the trick's clothes just for something fresh – plus he still owes me money – but what would I do with those clothes? I put on my own clothes, make some tea – Chester do you want any? Chester: that's his name. I make both teas and drink the rest of the juice, forget about the toast. Chester's all dressed up and shaven, with his bleached hair swept back he looks much younger. He grabs me around the waist and hugs me, which is what I like – he knows.

He says call me Monday and I'll give you what I owe you, I say great. I'm thinking what's going on, where is this leading me – he's kind of nice actually, I wouldn't mind some kind of situation. We kiss goodbye and I'm out the door, Fifth Avenue and there's the Plaza – so weird to walk outside and see that. I get a cab and head home, it's 6 when I get there.

At home I obsess about how I spend so much time focussing on eating healthy, relaxing, not putting toxins into my body – but I feel like a complete fucking disaster anyway. Then I do drugs and I don't really feel any worse – maybe a little edgier, that's all. Rina calls to see if I'm meeting her at Starlight women's night. I say honey I'm a mess, of course I'll be there. The idea of the subway's overwhelming so I call car service. As soon as I get to the bar, there's Rina with my first cocktail and then there's Sammie with some friends from Miami. I kiss everyone hello, it's great seeing Sammie out because she's got that groove. We're kinda shaking it in the aisle and Rina's got another cocktail already, she says taste this. I taste it and yum, what is it? A chocolate martini.

There's Marika – hey honey – I head for the bathroom, just gonna do a tiny bump of leftover coke.

That's what I needed, I step out and yes I'm *home*. There's Sammie with Rina, and wait, by the door there's Ian and Rashida. I want a repeat with Ian of the first time I saw him there, when I sucked his dick in the bathroom and swallowed all his come. I go over to them, and first thing Ian says is do you have any coke? I say not really, just a tiny bit. I take out one of the bags and feed a bump to each of them with a key, they both say thanks.

Then I get another cocktail and go over to the Miami children — there's this boy with all these piercings and a raver-goth aesthetic, so I know he isn't from here. Then there's a woman with long red hair and a deep tan, she keeps saying I remember you from...you know. I don't know. There's Rina with her gorgeous wool checkered floor-length skirt that she got from the Salvation Army in Clinton Hill for three dollars. My turn to buy drinks so I ask her if she wants another chocolate martini, so I go to the bar to get her one. Karen gives me another Stoli Vanilla on the rocks for free — how sweet; she tells me she loves my orange-striped French cuffs, which is quite the compliment because she's got style.

I give Rina her drink, she's swaying a little with the music, pointing out some woman she thinks is hot and I say you should go for Sammie. She's shaking her head no — it's in the family — but she would like to make out with her. I go back to Ian and Rashida on the bench, start making out with Ian and he's grabbing my dick. I'm biting and kissing, sucking on his neck and grinding into him. Then we're just holding hands and looking out.

Everything's *fine*. I go to the bathroom and there's Rina vomiting into the toilet and Sammie's massaging her back. I'm laughing — what's going on?

Then Rina's up but she's not so steady, Sammie's holding her and Rina says Mattilda will you take me home? I say no problem. I'm holding Rina and Sammie says bye dear, someone hands me Rina's purse and I tell Ian I'll be right back.

Rina stumbles out with me and says I'm not making a scene, am I? I say no honey don't worry about it, and we get into a cab. Rina's vomiting out the window and now I'm rubbing her back. We get to her corner, Rina gets out first and then falls flat on her back in the middle of the street. It's quite the glamour shot, but I say Rina, you've gotta get up, and I'm trying to pull her up but she's not helping. She says I'm fine.

I say Rina, you're in the middle of the street. Finally I drag her up and into her building, into the wood-paneled elevator, to her apartment door. While I'm trying to find the right key, Rina vomits on the floor—oh well. I get the door open and pull Rina in. Her apartment's a disaster—I mean a *disaster*. Everything is strewn across the floor, you can't even walk without stepping on a coat or the iron or a box of photos.

I get Rina to the bed and she says you can go. I say let me get your coat off, and we get it off. I say now your shoes, and pull them off. I say do you want to sleep with your clothes on? She says yes. I get her a big plastic bowl from the kitchen to throw up in, and then a glass of water with lemon. I grab the paper towels and head into the hallway to clean up the vomit.

I haven't cleaned up vomit in a long time and it's gross—chunky and smelly— yuck. Good thing I like Rina. I get it all up and hurry to throw the paper towels in the trash. Then I look for a snack, I need a snack—Rina's got nothing but tofu dogs so that'll have to do. They're actually not bad. I spot spirulina so I pour some into a glass of water, drink it but I'm still edgy—it's time for coke.

I go into the bathroom and do the rest of one bag, perfect. Then I write love you sweetheart on Rina's mirror with lipstick, kiss Rina goodnight, get outside and hail a cab. I get back to the bar and it's thinned out—women's night always ends early—Ian's still there and he says did you get any coke? I say no I was taking Rina home, wanna go to Dick's?

We go to Dick's and I give Ian the money for a forty—boom he's into the bathroom of course. Cokewhore. Then it's my turn, I do a bump and I'm wired—cocktails—and then I'm playing pool even though I don't know how to. Ian's flirting with some tacky boy in silver pants, I'm making faces at him and he motions me over when the boy goes to the bathroom. He says cute, huh—I say he's all right.

I go back to playing pool and I'm not as bad as I thought—the guy who I'm playing against is sexy, I say you want a bump, and I stick a key right under his nose. Then he gives me a bump, I say do you have any pot? He says is it okay if we smoke it right here in the bar, I say oh sure. I smoke some pot and there's the high I've been waiting for all weekend—I'm ready to get on the pool table, rip off my clothes and start dancing.

They're playing the craziest videos. First, it's showtunes, but '70s and '80s showtunes. There's one about someone dying and going to heaven—everyone gasps when it goes on but I don't know what it is. Then there's this Claymation version of "I Love New York," with a roly-poly Ed Koch singing all the lyrics. Is that really Ed Koch again?

Toby's the guy with the pot who's shooting his shot and I'm admiring his chest, my turn and then whoops last call. I go over to Ian — what do you want? He wants a screwdriver, I say the guy I'm playing pool with is hot, right. What about a foursome? Ian nods okay and I'm so high I'm about to flap my wings and fly around the bar. I pick up the cocktails and then there's more coke, more pot, I lose at pool but not by much. I'm leaning against Toby and this coke is good stuff, is that his boyfriend, what are we doing after this?

The bar closes and we're all heading to some afterhours — okay — it's freezing out and now we've got about eight people; luckily Toby has a car for four, the rest get into a cab. We head to some Italian restaurant on Bleeker with seven-dollar cocktails and what — no music, what's that all about? A bunch of straightboy cokeheads with a few fags, queens and women thrown in, sitting at the tables in an Italian restaurant. There's this one old-school leatherman with a high high-femme drag queen, who are they?

Ian's hitting on the silver-pants guy and there's Anita Cocktail, does she have pot? Great. I get her a cocktail. Then I head for the bathroom and there's Toby. We jump into a room, exchange bumps, and then we're making out. It's hot, grinding against the wall, oh I guess we'd better let the others in.

I go back to Ian and Anita; something's wrong so the place is closing already — Anita wants to go to her place but I'm going with Toby. We're last out the door, but then I realize that I've left my gloves and scarf, so I head back in. Look all around but no luck, just some straightboy who wants to hit on me for a bump of coke or a taste of my cock. I give him a bump and then I'm off, there's Ian and Anita but no Toby, shit where'd he go?

We head over to Anita's and I'm edgy, Anita pulls the I'll-get-out-and-you-pay number — which is fine because she's got pot. Then Ian does the same thing — that bitch needs to get read, but right now I've got money so I don't really care. We get to Anita's building and she says we can't go upstairs because my roommate's sleeping, but we can smoke pot down here. So then we're smoking pot right in front of the glass doorway to the building, somewhere in Hell's Kitchen I think — not so safe in terms of cops but whatever.

I pour a little coke into the bowl and then Anita and Ian don't want any more, which is fine 'cause soon I'm flying flying FLYING, don't even need those wings. Everything's suddenly red and we kiss Anita goodbye, jump into another cab, and I'm just letting my eyes roll back. When I open my eyes, Ian's saying something about how he shouldn't have smoked the pot, makes him too tired, and I say honey it's all about the pot, gliding over the bridge in the cab with the sun coming out it's WONDERFUL.

We get to my house and oh no I've lost my keys, someone must have kept them when I was giving out bumps. I call Jon five times but there's no answer. It's 7 o'clock; I figure someone must be getting up soon to go to work, so then at least we can get in the first set of doors. Ian's wrecked and we're both freezing, we walk back and forth for a bit and then Ian says I think I'm going to get the subway.

We kiss goodbye and now I'm crashing, go to Dunkin Donuts to use the bathroom and fuck they won't let me, even after I buy a bagel and tea. Now I'm a mess, I feel like my face is caving in and fuck if I hadn't lost my keys everything would be FINE.

The Sound of Rain

Microwave popcorn. It isn't popping enough and you can only feel the rain through the window if you press your lips against the glass.

The Rules

Warm-Up

It's finally spring, so of course I walk all the way across town to Stuyvesant Park. I swear I've got a hundred pounds of shit in my backpack, not to mention a shopping bag full of file folders and computer disks, but listen it's warm outside and there's no way I'm gonna miss the park. I get two blocks away and it starts to drizzle but who cares; I get to the entrance and suddenly I'm wired.

I walk right over to this couple in the middle, a guy in a blue warm-up suit or what do they call those stupid things. Jogging suits? Running suits? Whatever—he's with someone else but he's working me hardcore. I walk around but there's no one else I'm in the mood for, so I sit down next to a guy by the entrance who's not bad; I'd suck his dick. I say hi and he looks away, smokes a cigarette. After a few minutes he gets up and leaves. Bitch. I stay seated and the guy in blue walks over and I stare right at him and say hey. He says aren't you cold—because I've only got a t-shirt on—but I'm warm. He walks past me and then back, looks around and goes across the street to the other side of the park. Does he want me to follow?

I do one more go-around, but there's no one I'm hot for. I pass this older guy who's standing in the shadows, say hello and he's surprised—probably because no one's said a word to him. People are so damn rude in these places. I cross the street and there's the guy in blue right in the middle of the park getting blown by first one guy and then another. My heart's literally racing or maybe it's not my heart but whatever it is means I've got to get over there immediately or I might die.

I sit down right next to the guy in blue, he's got this huge, beautiful dick and one guy's on his knees sucking it. The third guy is grabbing the other guy's dick. The guy sucking takes a break so I lean over and take that beautiful dick in my mouth, then I get on my knees so I can get a better angle. The guy who was sucking grabs my dick, but I'm not hard yet, then the guy I'm sucking pushes my head down and his dick thrusts into my throat. It's too big and the force gets me hard and I'm gagging but wanting more and more, he's pushing my head all the way down and it's amazing, I'm hard and the other guy's sucking me.

Then I choke and some food comes up, I press back to breathe and the guy just pushes my head down, oh that amazing feeling, until finally I can't take it anymore, I push up hard and he releases. I swallow my vomit then go back down on the guy, put his hand on the back of my neck but then the other guy wants some, I sit up and the fourth guy — what's he been doing? — starts sucking my dick. Then the guy in blue says I'm gonna come and I put my hand on his abs to feel it, he comes in the guy's mouth and damn I want that come so bad.

The other guy gets up and starts spitting out the come, I wouldn't mind him spitting it into my mouth. Then the guy in blue gets up and I take his place, now my dick's looking large too — he looks back and I look him right in the eyes with heat. The fourth guy's still sucking my dick and the other guy's sitting next to me; I bend over and take his dick in my mouth, he pushes my head all the way down. His dick starts out medium but pretty soon he's huge too and I'm rock-hard in the fourth guy's mouth, though he's sort of hurting me.

I ask the guy whose dick I'm sucking to stand up and put his dick in my mouth. He hesitates, but then he's fucking my face, I pull his hand down to my neck and oh I'm so hard in the other guy's mouth, but I pull his head away so I don't come. I want the other guy to come in my mouth and I say so, but he already came — probably better that way for me anyway, I pull his head down and we start making out.

The guy who used to be the fourth guy — but now he's the third guy I guess — he's jerking my dick and I could come but I hold his hand to stop. I pull up my shirt and the third guy rubs my chest — yes — and I'm sucking the other guy's dick. Then he takes out his dick and starts smacking my face, he's grabbing my chest and holding my neck and the other guy's got a finger pumping at the edge of my asshole and his other hand jerking my dick. And I don't even know where I am anymore or what I'm doing and then I feel myself coming but I can't even tell if I've come yet, no there I'm coming no I've already come but my orgasm just goes on.

When I open my eyes, there's just me and the guy standing up and he grabs my head to make out but I'm coughing, a dryness in my throat like all this stuff is stuck there. I start laughing, it's spring yes it's spring and then I'm kissing the guy again and pulling up my pants, what's your name, his name's — now I can't remember — and I get up and there are guys wandering all over and good my bags are still there. I start walking and I'm coughing and laughing, I'm so high from coming, I'm walking down the street with my eyes sometimes rolling back and sometimes I'm just laughing, thinking how amazing sex can be, the insane high, how I need some throat lozenges.

Ten Dollars

Kyle calls me again, I thought his name was Jim so I tell him that and he thinks I'm playing with him. We met on a phone sex line, got off over the phone one night and since then he calls me about once a week to ask if I want to get together. When I told him I lived in Williamsburg, he said his favorite restaurant was Peter Luger's Steakhouse, which made me want to vomit. I could almost smell him, rancid cow blood oozing from his pores.

Kyle has this fantasy: wants me to come over and find him naked and blindfolded, piss in his mouth and then fuck him. He's never drunk piss and he's never been fucked, at least that's what he says. Kyle calls to chat for a few minutes, then starts talking about his fantasy until I get into it, today I'm in the bathroom and somehow he's got me ridiculously hard — it's his voice, kinda butch but sexier. Kyle wants me to go right over but I need to buy paint.

Kyle says what would it take to get you over here in twenty minutes and I say money, but that's not his fantasy so he ignores me. He wants me to tell him what else I'll do to him, but I don't have any ideas. Actually, I'm thinking about getting on my knees and sucking Kyle's dick, but I don't think that fits in with his plan.

Finally, I tell Kyle I'll come over at 6:30, but I've got to meet a friend for dinner at 7. Then Jon and I go to get paint and it's sort of warm out, maybe spring's really arriving. After a few blocks, though, I can feel the soot and the dust clogging my lungs, my eyes dry out and I talk about moving away from New York. Gotta get some fucking air.

Jon runs off with three gallons of paint so he

can do some work at home, and I go to the hardware store to copy keys. The hardware store smells like the inside of a gas tank, I keep picturing myself passed out on the floor with blood all over like Julianne Moore in *Safe*, before she was famous. Though *she* passed out at a dry cleaner's, so her clothes weren't ruined.

Finally the keys are ready and I go home, meditate so I don't pass out, eat, and then run out to meet Kyle. Kyle lives at Irving Plaza, which is this monstrosity of modern condos, organized like a maze. I get to his room and sure enough the door's open and he's naked on the bed with a blindfold and a baseball cap. I say hey, take my jacket off and straddle him, start to pull out my dick.

Kyle says what are you doing and I laugh, what does he think I'm doing? Then he says kiss me, so I kiss him and his whole body's shaking, he says hold me so I hold him and he's still shaking. I say are you okay? He says I'm a little nervous. I'm holding him and he says am I like I said, and I think no you're skinny and out of shape, but I say sure.

I'm holding Kyle and it feels nice, and then he's hard, he says let me look at you for just a second, just a peek and he pulls the blindfold down but I push it up. He says you're cute, and then I slide my dick into his mouth, I say you want me to piss in your mouth, but I'm already hard. I start fucking his face, then pull my dick out and he says what do you want? I put my dick back in his mouth, turn the baseball cap around and see that the middle of his head is all bald but I don't say anything. I say I'm too hard now to piss and he says what do you really want?

I want to leave soon, because I'm going to be

late to meet Laurie, but I move down until my dick's between Kyle's legs; he starts to hyperventilate, shaking again and he says hold me. I hold him and he's shaking; he says I'm so nervous and turned on, kiss me, and I kiss him, he says give me your tongue. My tongue goes all the way into his mouth and it feels good with Kyle sucking. I look down at Kyle's dick, hard, grab his balls and put his dick in my mouth. Up and down four times and Kyle's still shaking, then I can feel him starting to shoot so I move my mouth away, Kyle comes and a drop gets on my sweater; I wipe off the come and go to the bathroom to use Kyle's mouthwash and to piss.

Kyle says oh now you've gotta piss. I go back out and say it was cute when you were shaking, kiss him on the lips and say bye. I get downstairs and it's 6:59. I'll be seven minutes late. I feel energetic for the first time today, like holding Kyle lifted something out of me. Get to Angelica's Kitchen and there's Laurie, figure I'm making a glamorous entrance because I can feel my whole body in alignment and Laurie's laughing.

There are at least fifteen people waiting and Laurie says this reminds me of San Francisco. It's funny to think of it that way, a line in New York reminding you of San Francisco instead of the other way around. We sit outside to wait and it's cold but kind of refreshing.

I tell Laurie about Kyle and she gets confused, thinks Kyle's someone else from the phone line, someone I'm already friends with. Then Laurie thinks maybe I mean Gavin, since Gavin called last night, but Gavin actually works at Angelica's Kitchen in the take-out area, so we go in to say hi. Gavin asks if we want anything but Laurie's not hungry and I can't make up my mind, so we go back outside and pretty soon it's our turn for a table.

Laurie wants a Dragon Bowl, but I tell her everyone gets a Dragon Bowl—the specials are the best. So Laurie gets one special and I get the other, and Laurie gets sourdough bread even though I tell her it's all about the corn bread. I can't have either, since I'm allergic to wheat and corn again.

We get our food and it's good but something's wrong—it's not amazing. I eat every crumb anyway but Laurie leaves at least half of hers, but it's all wheat so I can't eat any. I complain about not getting any pages, hello am I a whore or what? Then I get a page but it's some flake. Laurie's food is still left, a chunk of green and beige and brown right in the middle of the plate.

Laurie orders dessert and they take her food away. Lemon tofu cheesecake, which is incredible—I had two bites of someone's once and it was almost too delicious. I have four bites of Laurie's and here comes my sugar crash, boom I'm shaky. We go outside and it's sleeting, so we get in a cab after waiting ten minutes.

We get to my house and I'm complaining about never getting any business and Laurie's sick of San Francisco and I'm sick of New York. Laurie wants to quit her job and I just want more energy, I want to date people, I want to have physical intimacy. Laurie likes New York and I hate it. Laurie takes a nap and then goes out to a bar.

Finally, at 3 a.m. I get a trick, and of course I don't want to go but I figure if I take this one then they'll all start calling me. The guy wants to fuck me, but hopefully I'll get out of it. I get to his house and he's coked out of his mind, can't get hard so I just keep sucking his dick, the bristles of his shaved pubic hair scraping my lips.

The trick decides to suck my dick and before you know it he wants to get fucked, and then I'm pounding him and he's loving it. I'm standing up while he's bent over on the bed, but I'm worried I'm going to slip on the waxed floor, so I lean onto him, and he says yeah fuck that ass yeah I want your load yeah and I'm kinda close to coming, usually I'd stop myself but the trick's saying I wanna see that load, so I figure why not let it out. Actually I'm picturing him inspecting the condom for sperm; he seems like the type. I'm fucking him harder and I can feel my orgasm starting even before I come, then after I shoot I still feel like I'm coming — such a great orgasm even with this annoying trick. Sometimes it just happens like that.

This trick's one of those guys who wants the full hour, so then I'm sucking his dick again and he's starting to get hard. Tells me he sees this guy Joey regularly and would I want to fuck Joey while he fucks me. I say sure, then it's time for me to go but the trick wants to fuck me now, I tell him not after I just came. Then he wants to get to know me, wants to know my real name. I tell him and he writes it down — why not if it'll make him call me back.

I figure this guy's going to tip, he had the money out from the beginning but now he wants to know if I have a ten for change. Cheap piece of shit. I just say no. Finally he gives me the one-sixty and says I'll owe him ten. Owe him ten, my ass.

Flats Fixed

When I turn my head to look back, he's already turned around, walking towards me with this grin on his face. Then I'm grinning too and one of us says what're you up to. Then I get confused. I start thinking maybe he just wants to talk, or maybe he thinks I'm someone else, or maybe he's straight. The straight thing's the worst, because the last three or four guys I've picked up have been straight. I mean, we've had sex, but I'm not into that drama.

So I'm hoping this guy's not straight and I'm telling him I'm on my way to buy t-shirts and he's from Albany, he's got two hours to kill before meeting a friend. He kind of talks straight, but he's definitely looking right into my eyes until our pupils lock and my vision gets all double so I have to blink a few times. I look at his hair, which is shaved off except in the center where it's dyed yellow. I think of talking about hair dye, but then I remember all of the times the most random people came up to me when I had dyed hair and talked about how they used to dye their hair. I don't want to be one of those random people. I say you can come over my place and we can have some fun.

People who live in Manhattan are bad enough at thinking Brooklyn's another country, but people from out of town sometimes think it's another world. This boy — Brent's his name — think's it's too far, but I tell him I live in Williamsburg, we can just hop on the L and it's only four stops. Ten minutes. Brent says oh I don't know, so then I get self-conscious again, thinking maybe he doesn't want to sleep with me after all. I tell him I'll show him where Barnes & Noble is, he was looking for it before he found me.

We turn around and I'm trying to figure out whether Brent's a fag. Then he says do you know of anywhere around here where we could go, and I look at his eyes, I say you mean a bathroom? He smiles and I lean over and grab him and say we're *definitely* going to have to get together again. I say most of the bathrooms around here are going to be too crowded, there's a peepshow but they've been cracking down. Then there are some sex clubs but they're awful. We could try Barnes & Noble.

We walk towards Barnes & Noble and Brent's asking me about cruisy areas and I'm thinking of all the places we can have sex in the future if this turns out well. We walk inside and Brent says do you know of anywhere where people hustle? I pause for emphasis, and almost laugh. I say do you hustle. He says well every now and then, and there's that grin again. I say that's what I do for a living. We walk upstairs to the bathroom and the security guard walks in right in front of us. Brent shakes his head and leaves the bathroom, but I have to piss.

When I get out of the bathroom, Brent's waiting, which is a good sign because I was having visions of him running away. Then he says well we better go back to your place because otherwise I'm going to waste all my time thinking about it, and there's the grin that makes me sweat. We walk towards the subway station and he says I'm kind of embarrassed, but I already have to borrow money from my friend to take the train home, do you have an extra subway token? I say don't worry about it.

We get on the subway and I'm sitting down while Brent is standing up; I'm studying his face to see how cute he is, and he's cute. I'm thinking it'll be funny when I tell Steve this story because he was obsessed with a guy named Brent for years. Even followed him to Germany. But this Brent's following me, and I'm definitely excited because I'm sick of having sex only with tricks who are paying or with guys at sex clubs or straightboys in parks. We get to my stop and I want to put my arm around Brent, but the last time I did that, he made it into something weirdly straight, so I'm not sure if he's comfortable with public affection.

We walk out and I say well here we are in glamorous Williamsburg, and he tells me how the only other time he's been to Brooklyn was the last time he was in New York, and he thinks that time it was Park Slope. I say I wouldn't mind living there — queers and a park and cruising — but I'll probably never move because I've got a huge loft space and my rent's so cheap and Park Slope's pricey. Besides, Seventh Avenue in Park Slope is like the dumping ground for rejects from *The Real World*.

I tell him about the different parts of Williamsburg: the ridiculously hip part about twenty minutes away, the Italian part, the Hasidic part, and the Latino part where I live, which is mostly warehouses and subsidized housing and car repair shops with signs that say Flats Fixed. I used to think Flats Fixed meant they'd fix up people's apartments, which seemed like a weird thing to see advertised around here. But not totally unlikely, I mean I wouldn't mind having my flat fixed.

Brent's craving a cigarette, I tell him I'll buy him a pack if we can't find someone to bum one from, and he gets all smiley, he says I'll make you come twice if you buy me a pack. I can tell that Brent's used to working people for little things, but it doesn't bother me yet. We go into the store and someone's saying something about faggots, I figure he means us.

We get to my building and Brent smokes while we look at the Bell Atlantic power station or whatever that is across the street. We get inside my apartment and walk to the back and take off our coats and I kiss Brent and we start to make out. I'm actually into the cigarette taste, which surprises me since I really can't stand smoking anymore. Then Brent says can I give you a massage, I say sure and I'm wondering if he doesn't want the intimacy of kissing. I lay down on the bed and Brent gets on top of me, he starts to massage my shoulders but he isn't too good at it, all fast and jerky. Then he moves down my back, lies on top of me and I can feel his hard-on through my pants, poking at my asshole.

Cowboy Boots

My fingers brushed against his hand as I took the pen from under the stall; I wanted to grab onto his thighs. The note said, "I don't know where the stairwell is." Fuck. I wrote, "Follow me," and passed back the pen. His message was ready: "OK." I breathed. I heard wheels in the hallway, the bathroom door swung open and the janitor came in. I unrolled some toilet paper and pretended to wipe, flushed the toilet. Pulled up my jeans and tried to hide my hard-on with my sweater but that didn't work. I opened the stall door and went over to the sink, washed my hands.

I nodded when he walked over to the mirror, pulled out a paper towel. He was actually cute — I couldn't keep myself from smiling. I left the bathroom and walked over to the pay phones, tried to hide the bulge in my pants by turning toward the wall. He followed me, I caught his eye and walked past the elevators, into the stairwell. The door swung closed and then open; he was right behind me. I hurried downstairs. We got to the last parking level and there was a chain blocking us from going further. I was sweating.

He stopped beside me, said do you live nearby? He didn't know how old I was. I looked at my watch, what's today? Wednesday. I could smell his mouthwash: Scope. Wednesday. My father wasn't in his office. I said okay, just a few blocks away. We walked back into the mall. I kept hoping I wouldn't run into anyone from school. We walked out the side door, across the street, downhill, right, uphill, into the building. I glanced over to make sure he was still with me. He was. The guard smiled and buzzed me in, did he know?

I pushed the elevator button and stared at it. The elevator stopped, we got in and I pressed the button. Did the guard know? What would I do if he told my father? The elevator doors opened, I saw myself next to this guy in the mirror. He was my height, with reddish hair and a brown leather jacket. When we got to the apartment, I unlocked the door and held it open, turned on the lights and he sat down on the analytic couch. He said do you live here? He slid off his cowboy boots. I said no, it's my father's office. I dropped my backpack and pulled off my shoes. He was unbuttoning his shirt, I could see his pale skin and freckles, red chest hair. I was used to bathrooms, I didn't know what to do. Come here, he said, and I sat down next to him. Lie down. I lay down and he got on top of me, I gasped. I felt like I was about to come already.

He slid his hands under my sweater and I giggled. What's wrong? Nothing, I'm just ticklish. He sat up and took off his shirt. I reached through his pants for his dick. He was hard. He reached over and pulled off my t-shirt and sweater as I lifted my hands. I bent over and started licking circles around his nipples, like I read about in this sex guide I got from the *Adam and Eve* catalog. I watched his freckles. He grabbed my dick through my pants, I squeezed his dick harder. I looked up at him, his eyes were bright blue. I wanted to kiss him. I looked back down.

He unbuttoned my pants, I leaned back as he unzipped them and pulled them off with my boxers. I was glad I wasn't still wearing briefs. He started licking my balls and I leaned back onto the couch. I was trying not to come yet. He pulled on my cockhead with his lips, then sat up and took off his jeans. I put one hand under his balls, leaned over and slid his cockhead into my mouth, but I didn't really know what to do. Usually the guys I met were old men and I didn't want to suck their cocks.

His crotch smelled like Dial. He leaned back so I guessed I was doing okay, but I didn't want to get AIDS so I sat up and reached for his dick, he reached for mine. His pointed straight out, mine was bigger but I hated the way it curved, made it look like I couldn't get all the way hard. We both leaned back onto the couch. I grabbed one of his thighs, just below his balls. I spit on my other hand and started jerking him off. He was teasing my cockhead with two fingers, then he grabbed my whole dick and started jerking fast. I was trying not to come before he did. I jerked faster and he started to breathe more heavily, then he came, squeezed my dick harder and I came.

Do you have a towel, he said and I pulled on my boxers and went into the kitchen for a roll of paper towels. When I got back, he was already buckling his belt. He said I got some on the couch, sorry. I said oh, don't worry about it. He wiped it up and asked what he should do with the towel. I put it on the desk. I pulled on my jeans, then my t-shirt and sweater. He was putting on his boots, I'd always hated cowboy boots but right then I wasn't so sure. I stared at his boots so I'd remember them if I saw him in the bathroom. I wondered if he was a Republican — Democrats don't wear cowboy boots. I wondered how old he was, how old did he think I was? He sat up, thanks. I asked him his name: David. I'm Matt. I looked him in the eyes. He looked down, said I better be going.

He left, and I didn't feel disgusted like usual.

I wanted to run after him and hold him in my arms, kiss him and say I love you, look him in the eyes for a long time. I couldn't remember his name.

Teeth on Backwards

Kids at school would call him Aquafresh, Colgate, Crest. Trina called him Tampax 'cause everyone knew you had to use ob. Soon the other kids caught on; they'd call him Tampafresh. Or Colgax. He'd bite his tongue and taste it, when they played Greek dodge he'd dodge.

Slowly, he learned to laugh: performance art. He'd hide in the bathroom to breathe. If only home wasn't shit.

Old Enough

Maybe I go home with Lawrence because of the symmetry: he graduated from college in the same year I was born. "Old enough to be my father" isn't the phrase I would use, though I count the years between us and he would need another eight. He says you're too old for me.

When I go to get another beer, Lawrence takes my space against the wall. I say we can share, and I touch his stomach which is hard. He asks me what gym I go to.

I watch the boy who's turning me on. With Lawrence I'm confident because I imagine his desire shapes mine. When we leave, Lawrence notices someone outside who swings around to look me in the eyes. Lawrence says you got checked out. Then the boy turns around again, I say should I go after him? Lawrence says that's your decision and he brushes his hand against my dick.

Then the boy looks back again and Lawrence says that's three times. Lawrence kisses me and grabs my dick and by then the boy is a block away. I say he'd probably think I was mugging him. Lawrence says you can come home with me and we start walking.

Lawrence's dick is exactly the same size as my dildo, only flesh-colored instead of blue. Actually, Lawrence's dick is longer than my dildo and his cockhead is bigger, but I make the comparison. Lawrence grabs my head when I suck his dick and I gag a little, which is how I like it, and when he starts to pump my face I get hard.

Lawrence fucks my face but this isn't porn. When we move to the bed, Lawrence wants to wrestle and actually that's fun, though my legs get tired because I've been doing nothing but walking for the last few weeks. Lawrence says you're strong—all lean and toned—and when he tries to flip me over I let him.

I want Lawrence to fuck me, but I can tell he isn't going to get hard enough to make it easy. I try to fuck Lawrence, but the condom makes me lose my erection. Then Lawrence comes all over my chest and my yellow come mixes with his white come and I wish I'd swallowed it all. Maybe this is porn.

When I wake up, I have the bed to myself in this huge loft space like something out of *Architectural Digest*. The cleaning service is there too. I eat puréed squash and kiss Lawrence goodbye, he walks me into the elevator and I think he wants to make out.

The Rules

I've been dancing in front of the NO DANCING sign for at least an hour — practically by myself — but finally people are joining me. This one boy starts doing these great slow moves, leaning back in exaggerated poses, and I'm looking him in the eyes and making faces. He comes over, but only to mouth the words of the song, and then he's dancing slow with another boy — maybe his boyfriend — and I'm staring at him and laughing flirtatiously. Finally he comes over again, he says you look sweaty. I say I'm not leaving until they give me the NO DANCING sign, and I can't hear what he says. He says Frank louder and kind of spits, and then he says it three more times, and now he's kind of in my arms and I say kiss me. He kisses me once and then goes off to talk to someone else.

I catch Douglas walking to the back, haven't seen him in months. I grab him and we give each other a hug, I say you going into the backroom? He says is that what's back there? I've had a crush on Douglas for at least a year, and there's definitely something mutual going on, but he won't sleep with me because I'm a whore. Though if he's going into that backroom, then he's gonna have some explaining to do.

I go back to dancing, I'm covered in sweat and everyone's staring at the go-go boy. I mean, it's true that this guy's hot as hell and he's got a huge dick, but he's there every fucking week, doing the same thing. Everyone's got their eyes wide and some guys literally have their mouths open, gaping. No one's tipping, though — too embarrassed or cheap — if they're gonna stare like that, they really should shell out the bucks. Plus, the go-go boy is Latino and practically everyone in the audience is white — racial fetishism in all its glory — New York, New York.

Peter comes over to tell me that he and Harvey are going to the new bar — what new bar? — on Avenue B — but I want to keep dancing. Peter says wait for me, I've got your stuff in my car. I keep dancing, every now and then someone's staring at me instead of the go-go boy, but I can't decide whether I'm horny. I'm just loving the fact that I'm dancing, haven't danced in so fucking long. Can't quite get centered and I'm wondering if it's my new boots. Candis Cayne comes on stage for her show; it's exactly the same as her earlier show, down to the pulling off of her hair clip, swinging her hair around, turning to fall against the wall, tugging her dress down to show us her new tits. Some guys are teasing her with a dollar bill and that just gets me angry, I want to smack the fuckers but instead I just tip Candis a five. She holds it up for the audience to see and then the show's over.

I go to the back and look for Douglas, I'm leaning over people but I can't find him. Guess he actually went into the backroom. Then he stands up and we talk, one of his friends leaves so we sit on the sofa and Douglas' eyes are fixated on the backroom. I say I thought you were back there, but he says no nothing exciting like that ever happens to me. I say you could make it happen. He says I haven't had sex in six months, and I say you can have sex with me. He says then I'll have to pay you two hundred dollars, which is the same thing that every tacky middle-to-upper class fag who I don't know always says, so I'm disappointed in Douglas. I say no I'll have sex with you for free.

Douglas just smiles so I figure that's a no, but it's not uncomfortable or anything. We talk and then he says I think I'm going to check it out, will you watch my jacket. I laugh and then Douglas' friend comes back—Kevin—he's cute too. I say you won't believe where Douglas just went, Kevin says where and I point. We're talking for a few minutes and all these hot boys are going back, Kevin goes back there and says will you watch my jacket?

Frank comes out of the backroom, I say what were you doing back there without me? He says I was looking for my friend. Who does she think she's kidding? Frank sits down and I'm rubbing his chest, kind of holding him, and I say kiss me and then we're making out and Douglas and Kevin are back. Kevin says you're bringing the backroom out here. Frank goes to look for his friend and then Douglas and Kevin want me to watch their jackets, I say you're not leaving me here again. So Douglas, Kevin, Frank, and I go to the back.

It's more crowded than I've ever seen it— wall-to-wall bodies and you can't even move. We're trying to get somewhere, everyone's pushing but no one's really doing anything. The energy's stuck. I lean back and kiss Kevin on the neck. I say I don't know what to do because I came in here with the three hottest boys in the bar. Everyone's kind of motionless, inside and outside I think. Or nervous and high, I don't know. Someone's grabbing my dick and someone's pushing my ass, is one of those people Douglas? If he wants to have sex with me, he's gotta say so. Douglas and Kevin push forward and I'm left alone, who knows where Frank is.

I get to the back corner and there's Kevin, I say hey and kiss him on the neck again. Then we're making out and Frank's grabbing me from behind, saying I thought we were married. I say we can all be married. Kevin's grabbing my dick through my pants, so I'm feeling his dick and he's hard, he's unzipping my pants so I unbutton his pants and then I get on my knees. I'm sucking his dick and then something happens to make me stand up, it's too crowded or maybe it's Frank making a lot of noise. Kevin says I'm gonna go out, it's just too much.

I go back into the crowd and I'm not really horny, just looking for someone to turn me on, but really everyone's just standing around. One guy's hugging me and it feels good, but then I turn around and it doesn't feel so good anymore. Funny how sight changes touch, though really why should it? I run into Peter and then I see some guy fucking someone's face; my whole mood changes. Watching the guy getting sucked sends this surge from my groin through my body and I'm shaking inside. I press my hand on his chest and he's moaning and I'm so hot from watching him and I'm grabbing his dick at the base, and then the guy on the ground stops sucking, so I bend down.

Tastes like he just came, but he's hard so I keep sucking anyway, then stand up after a few minutes because maybe he's trying to zip up his pants. Now I'm just craving another dick in my mouth, like someone from a porno called *Cock Crazed* or *Hungry Pussyboy*. Sometimes I wonder why I like sucking cock so much. I grab one guy's dick through his pants and then he takes it out and I'm back on my knees; it's like one motion the two of us together.

This guy's got a great dick, I feel up his body to see what that's like—he's got hard pecs but a soft stomach. Really I don't care that much what he looks like, that's what's fun about backrooms — you forget who you're touching and everyone's a chain of sexual action and reaction. But then sometimes, like tonight, it's everyone standing around trying to figure out what everyone else looks like, waiting for someone to start something.

I've definitely started something and then there are three or four hands grabbing the guy's dick, one then the other. One guy's jerking him into my mouth or maybe that's him, I don't know. I just want his dick, I'm fighting with the hands and then I've got his whole dick for a while and I'm unbuttoning his pants. The lights are starting to come on and the crowd's thinning a little, I stand up and the guy who I was sucking moves his dick right to someone else's mouth, some old guy sitting on the side. I think he's choosing *him* over me, what's that about? So there I am making those same judgments.

I look around and there's Stewart Bank, one of my tricks. I say hi Stew. He says I didn't realize you were so close, but I didn't even realize he was at the bar, so I figure he was watching me. I kiss him and he says are you okay, I don't know what he means. I say I'm fine, I sit down and he goes out. The lights in the back are on now, but not yet in the backroom, and Mario comes back to say okay gentlemen wrap it up.

The backroom's kind of disturbing tonight, it's like even when guys are having sex there's no connection; they're watching tv. Everyone's in a frenzy or dead. The two guys whose dicks I sucked didn't even acknowledge me. Sometimes it's different, a community of gestures. Frank comes over, says you were naughty, I say rub my chest while I jerk off okay, and he's just kind of touching me, not looking at my dick, which is strange, and then I come—finally a release—I button my pants just as the backroom lights go up.

I walk out and there are Douglas and Kevin on the sofa, I tell Douglas I think I freaked Kevin out, even though it's Kevin's drama not mine. Douglas says yeah. I sit down and Kevin says just tell me you don't have oral herpes, I say no I'm a responsible slut, and kiss him while he turns his mouth away. He says good, because otherwise I'd be worrying all night. Peter's motioning for me to go, but I say wait. Frank comes over, I say kiss me, he says I know where your mouth has been. I say are you gonna give me your number? He says I want someone tonight, you got off now what am I going to do?

I say pick someone up, he says what, for sloppy seconds? He's already annoying me, I say do you want to give me your number, I can always use new friends. He starts to give me his number and Harvey yells from the front that he already has it. I say oh my friend already has it, and Frank looks around, who's your friend? Harvey. I don't know any Harvey.

I walk over to Peter at the bar, I say I just got in a mess, it's drama here tonight. There's a drag queen who says she just came from the Tunnel and it's more drama there, I say I mean a different kind of drama—sex drama. She says well that sounds better than Jersey drug drama. I say I don't know. I start to tell everyone the story, but the management's trying to get everyone out. Peter's talking to the bartender though, so we're okay. I start to tell the story, but then we start to leave.

I get outside and there's Douglas again, I hug him and say do you want to go to Body and Soul on

Sunday? He says no, but the next time you go. I say I never go, because no one will ever go with me. Kevin looks uncomfortable and I'm thinking that bitch is a mess. I kiss Harvey goodbye—he's all friendly now, which is nice. Then I get in Peter's car and I feel like we've definitely just had a night. He says do you want me to come over, I say let's just sleep at our own homes tonight. He says yeah you've already had sex anyway, which I don't really understand because we don't have sex, just sleep together every now and then. He says you'd at least have to take a shower.

I'm sick of everyone giving me shade. It's like one bitchy comment after the other—there was a time when I would have read everyone, but now I just smile. I do the same thing when someone calls me faggot on the street: photo-op. I mean, that whole bar exists just so there's somewhere to get it on. Usually I go right to the backroom, but tonight I went up to the guys I was hot for, and look what happened. I'm all annoyed, I say I guess I made the mistake of bringing people into the backroom who I'd already met—that's against the rules.

Aliens

Falling in Love with Francis

Something CLICKS in me when I see Francis' sign, maybe I'm being naive and all, but I think it might just be true love or at least what they call something to write HOME about, though I have to admit I'm confused about where home is:

a. watering the plants in East Boston
b. diving into Lake Washington
c. getting high from dancing

But back to TRUE LOVE I mean Francis: I'm in an ice cream shop on Avenue A but I'm vegan so I don't eat ice cream. I look at the signs on the bulletin board and FEMALE MODEL WANTED pops out at me, mostly because of the road trip around the world and wondering how we'd drive around the entire world, not just from New York to San Francisco and back. I've done that — I'm looking for new adventures and yes LOVE and today they have coconut sorbet at the ice cream parlor and it's vegan. But I can't eat anything with too much sugar or I get so sketchy my life becomes one big breakdown. I don't get any sorbet — I get Francis.

Now some of you might think that Francis doesn't sound like a French name, but listen I'm not looking for AUTHENTICITY, I want love. Sure I'm skeptical, but it's something about how Francis puts anarchy and peace and artist together at the bottom of the page that makes me fall for him. It's not many people who make those CONNECTIONS.

So I call Francis, we make an appointment for Sunday at noon. He lives in a penthouse at Red Square on Houston Street. I've always wondered what kind of people live there. Once someone who lived there gave me a dead plant, but when Francis fucks me it isn't like porn or real life, his dick just slides in. Then I think wait a second; what am I doing getting fucked again without a condom by someone who I'm not attracted to when he isn't even paying me? I sit right up and when I speak to Francis I'm speaking to every guy who's ever just slid it in without asking. Foreplay isn't the same thing as CONSENT. And with Francis it's even more complicated than the wholesale acceptance of objectification in gay male sexual culture. Because Francis isn't gay. He's some straight French painter who just wanted a female model and instead he got me.

But when I speak to Francis I can't speak. This isn't some straight-acting fag, this is the real thing. When I pull away from him, he says you look like Linda Blair in *Poltergeist*. I just stand there speechless because Linda Blair wasn't in *Poltergeist* and here I am in the penthouse of Red Square with a view of the Brooklyn Navy Yard, trying to tell Francis that I just don't love him anymore.

I go home and get dressed. I pull on my jellybean tights with a women's bathing suit from the '60s: green palm trees on white. Then I put two curly wigs in for tits. I step into my plaid stack heels and grab the shower curtain rings out of the bathroom to make a choker. Throw on about fifty fake pearl necklaces, and big dangly plastic crystal earrings. Then I smear eyeliner from my eyes to my nose and lipstick from my lips to my chin. Finish the outfit with old lady cockroach sunglasses and a shower cap that has big plastic flowers growing off it.

I look in the mirror and something is missing. I pull out another wig for pussy hair. I have a big dilemma about that part, I keep thinking is this misogynist? In the past I would have thought yes, but sometimes I think I'm a '70s lesbian feminist, like how I used to believe all penetrative sex was rape. Then I realized I'd been raped by my father and that was why, how my biggest fear wasn't being raped because that was to be expected. How my biggest fear was ever being in a position where I could be the rapist. I'm still scared to take a self-defense class because then I have to be the aggressor.

I call car service. I say Saks Fifth Avenue and when I get there I walk in like I own the place, go right into couture. Look at a few price tags and start screaming I THOUGHT THIS WAS A THRIFT STORE. I can't get any help. I wipe my makeup off on a powder pink Chanel suit, then go down to cosmetics screaming LIPSTICK, grab a few testers and smear them across my face, rubbing them into the floor as they break off. At this point, there are a few people staring. I pull off my shower cap, take out the pussy wig and move it to my head, adjust it in the mirror and say *it's all about glamour.*

Showing Me

You stretch to the sky like a pole and then squat to the ground like a mushroom: one of those mirrors in a fun house. I can't digest anything. When you look at me, I turn to stone. That's how I know you're my mother.

Piss

My father would unlock the bathroom with scissors while I was in the shower, I'd scream GET THE FUCK OUT. He and my mother had their own bathroom. He'd chuckle and say I just had to piss. It took me years to say that word he made me so sick. We had a glass shower door that distorted everything in the shower but it was still translucent, I never knew how much of me my father could see. I'd cover my crotch with a sponge until he left. Our bath mats were made of shag carpet, different shades of light green stained and matted. I remember where we got the rugs, in the shopping center with Goldman's Deli and Loehmann's, the shopping center where my parents saw *An Officer and a Gentleman*. Later, I'd lie naked on the bathroom floor, grinding my dick into the rug by the sink and pressing my face into the rug by the toilet until I came, surrounded by the smell of my father's piss.

Aliens

She's busy devaluing her art, wants the creditors to say what is this junk? Later, the critics will say, "Using the contrasting color palette of minerals and plants, Rose Stern paints supernatural landscapes without a tree in sight." And, "Rose Stern personalizes the abstract." She hasn't had a show in years, wants her family to inherit something worthless so that, later — after she's famous — they'll become rich.

I want to ask Rose silly questions like how do you see yourself in the context of twentieth century art? She says I'm much better than Jackson Pollock... I'm not as good as Mark Rothko because he did something different. I'm like Richard Diebenkorn, only maybe he was a better painter. But there are things I can do that I don't think anyone else can.

Rose likes everything about cabbage except the smell of it. I don't tell her about the trick who had me drop cabbages on his stomach, one by one, until I said enough already — the story is supposed to be about oranges. The next time we met, he kneeled on the ground with his dick on a piano bench, hard. I stood on his dick with all my weight, in combat boots, amazed at what the human body can take and relaxed by it.

My father played the piano for years, he'd practice until his fingers fell off and then people would say you have the hands of a piano player and he'd practice more. It's his eyes I remember; when he took off his glasses I'd scream, like in Rose's portrait of him, "The eyes of her son stare out like horses eyes." I fell in. In Rose's house, the paintings sing. The critics say: "catapult."

Rose tells me about a friend of hers, a young

guy, a personal trainer — very handsome, and so nice — in his forties and not married, Rose wanted to fix him up. He said I'm gay, I asked for the point of the story. The point, Rose says, is that I didn't even know he was gay; I can't stand your earrings.

I go to the gym at the Jewish Community Center, it's the first time I realize that the JCC is like the Y. I went to a JCC for a little while for Hebrew school, but all I remember are the crayons and the construction paper. I tell Rose I felt like an alien. I say it's like I dropped you off for a few hours at a nursing home in Wyoming, but Rose doesn't understand what it means to be straight. She doesn't understand that Baltimore for me is how I imagine Wyoming would be for her, that I'm more out of place at the JCC than she would be at a nursing home.

Maybe Rose is too practical to know what it's like to be an alien. She says, contained in almost all my paintings, there are three or four other paintings that I'm wasting. When Rose hears the hurricane approaching, she goes outside to water the plants. She brings in a leaf, taste this. Chocolate mint.

Rose tells me how, years ago, when she was a camp counselor, she saw a little girl get killed by a school bus. Years before Rose's car could get stolen from outside her house, or the guy next door would get killed. When Rose says: by a hustler — you know this isn't a John Waters film, because the garden in the background is landscaped.

Rose knows how to choose her words. She says maybe I'll have my friend the trainer take you to the gym. Stuck at my grandmother's house for even a few days, I crave the sight of another fag. Rose says *if* you take off those earrings. It's a battle I can't win, I go on strike anyway. Rose says to me: I spent a year trying to make a white that was warm enough for the sun.

Runway

I decide that today my depression will end, but it all depends on the Ear, Nose, and Throat clinic. They're going to clean out my ears and I'm going to hear cigarette ashes falling on asphalt. But then the doctor looks into my ears and says there's no wax, we need to wait two months to see if you'll need surgery. That just fucks up my plan. I thought I was going to leave the clinic doing runway, and instead I leave thinking I'm dying.

The dying part happens because the doctor gives me some anesthetic up my nose so he can stick this little camera in and look around. Good thing I'm not as paranoid as some of my friends. The anesthetic makes me nauseous. I feel like I'm going to pass out right there, lying on the floor unable to hear anything. Then the doctor says do you have any risk factors for HIV, I mean what kind of question is that? I say sure, he says well this could be HIV-related.

He might as well say you've got the fag's virus sucking up your hearing like a Slurpee. I leave thinking no one's ever come in my ass; I've swallowed come, but maybe it was that time someone shot in my eye. Later on, I decide to go to the Boiler Room for a beer. I never go there because everyone's working that cult of masculinity thing, but for some reason I suddenly have this idea that I'll meet my dreamboy there. I get a Bass Ale and squeeze a bunch of lemon in it to keep my electrolytes balanced. I drink the beer SLOWLY — over a whole hour and that's good, makes me kind of happy and calm.

But the bar is boring, nothing happening and hardly anyone to cruise and my dreamboy just doesn't show up. To tell you the truth, I'm not even looking for my dreamboy; I just want to fall asleep in some guy's arms. 2 a.m. comes around and I don't want another beer so I go over to the Bijou, even though I'm not that horny, just unfulfilled. Before I left Seattle, I thought a sex club couldn't get any worse than Basic Plumbing, but Basic Plumbing was like heaven compared to the Bijou. The Bijou is worse than a bar, at least at a bar people talk a little and laugh and sort of have fun. At the Bijou, people just walk around in circles looking dazed.

Everyone waits for a cubicle to open up because this is crackdown time and there won't be sex in any public space *inside* a fucking sex club. In every cubicle, there's some worn-out guy with a vacant, dazed look on his face. Some guys will hog a cubicle for hours. Not that I'm all excited about getting in on that action; I go to a sex club to get on my knees and suck five guys' cocks, to fuck some guy against a wall while someone else is eating my ass and I'm making out with a third guy who's got his hands around my neck. But not at the Bijou.

If there's a cure for horniness, it's the Bijou. Ten minutes there and I want to go home and go to bed. But of course I wait. I try to talk to a few guys and they can't deal. So I wait. I mean—no question about it—I'm one of the hottest guys there by just about anyone's standards, but nothing is happening for me. I try to go into a cubicle for a threesome, but the cubicle-holder won't have it. I tell myself I'll leave by 3. Then I say after I go to the bathroom and get hard at the urinal to see if I can start something. But I'm so bored that I can't even get hard.

3:30 comes around and I'm still there. I figure I better get something out of this place so I take all the condoms from a basket and put them in my pocket. Twenty-three Kimonos, so I guess that's worth the ten-dollar cover plus seventy-five cents for a locker. I leave that dump wanting to SCREAM, thinking just take me back to my empty apartment where I don't have to deal with any of this shit. I find a good luck penny in the cab because I sure need some.

When I get home, I put on Armand Van Helden's *Witch Doktor* cd and that brings me right back to Boston. I know it's bad when I start thinking about Boston. Ritchie would play a runway song and the floor would clear, all the black queens would come out and walk, and sometimes the clubkids too though usually we'd just screech and yell work *mama*, make space for the queens and turn it out on the sidelines. Ivari would walk out like a three-hundred-pound tranny supermodel, waving her fan with letters that spelled it all out: I-V-A-R-I. We'd all be saying *walk* for me, and the queens would walk. I liked Deena the best, she'd walk back and forth all night fanning herself with a handkerchief and somehow that just sent me to the sky. None of that RuPaul hips-to-the-walls sort of thing, just a subtle swing.

But anyway I get back from the Boiler Room, take off all my clothes, put on my gold house boxers and black stacks, and I just use that room like I'm living large. First I'm practically stomping across, witch *doktor*, shrieking and laughing, throwing up my right leg and doing my special fly-through-the-air-and-twist-around, crowd-stopping move. Then I switch to the Fugees version of "Killing Me Softly," and I slow down and do runway like my life depends on it. Because it does.

Hypoglycemia

Macrobiotics

Everyone else is ready to leave, and I know I should go too but it's been months since I've had a cocktail and one just isn't going to do it. At least once a day, I crave cocktails so badly that my eyes roll back and I know that really I need to eat. But tonight I've just eaten, so I think what the hell. I bring organic blue corn chips into the bar with me so I'll stay grounded. But after that first cocktail, I want to get to that point when I can't do anything but lean against the wall and feel my head moving diagonally upwards and back. I get another cocktail; this one's literally clear, and when I take the first sip I get that rush like *here I am*. But thinking sip it, drink it slowly, savor it. And eating my blue corn chips.

Then I start thinking about drugs, waiting for someone to offer me a bump of something. Knowing I'll regret it afterwards but thinking I just want to be *high*. Then I get a third cocktail, still sipping it and thinking this is so fucking delicious. Either I need sex or drugs, and sex is safer — sex will get me out of here and then I won't think about drugs. But I'm so incompetent at cruising bars, I get all worried about whether some guy's really cruising me or is he cruising that empty space right next to me?

I finish my cocktail and sit down on the sofa by the wall, this guy sits next to me and he isn't really cute but we start making out. He tells me his name is Javier and he's French and last night he tried coke for the first time but mostly he just likes drinking because alcohol makes him happy. I say I don't usually do drugs — anymore — but I want to say GIVE ME SOME K. Javier buys me a drink and then asks me to go home with him but I'm thinking here I go again sleeping with some guy who I'm not attracted to because I'm too scared to cruise someone who makes me hot.

I say I need to dance, do you want to go to Life? I'm trying to decide whether I actually want k or whether it's the alcohol and it doesn't really matter because I've just finished my fourth cocktail. And once I've had four cocktails, it's over for me. I sip at the ice and convince myself that I'd definitely decide to do drugs even if I hadn't had anything to drink.

I'm out of money, and Javier offers to pay for Life, but I need k so we take a cab back to my apartment in Williamsburg and I get money. Javier keeps trying to grab my dick and by this point I'm not into him at all. I don't want sex anymore, I just want to walk out of the bathroom stall after doing a bump and go onto the dance floor when the music gets three times louder and I start sinking into the ground and my mouth hangs open and my eyes keep shifting in and out of focus and all I can think is *yes*.

We get to Life, right as we walk in the door I see Ian, I lean over to kiss him and he says *I'm out of my mind.* I say I'm looking for k, he says you and everyone else, and then he runs off somewhere. Javier leans over to kiss me and I say I think I'm going to wander around.

I look for who's got that dazed k'ed-out look in their eyes or who looks like they know the sources or who just looks friendly. First I ask the ravey boy with the lycra camouflage shirt and the wrap-around sunglasses, but he's from out of town—though he's got acid and he'll throw me a hit if I find k. I end up sending out four or five scouts, but they keep circling the club and not finding anything.

Finally I ask someone by the bathroom and

he laughs and points to both of the guys next to him. I get a forty-dollar vial and rush into a stall to do a bump. I find the boy with acid and I say I've got k. I give him a big bump and he gives me a tab of acid, which I put right under my tongue. Then I find this boy Stephen who was looking out for me, and we go into the bathroom. He says do you want a bump of coke, and we trade. Then I'm standing by the dance floor a little bit out of it, but not high enough, dancing with this woman who seems fun. I lean over and say *you* look like you need a bump of k. She smiles and we go into the bathroom. She says do you want some tina and I say you don't have coke, do you?

Then I end up doing a tiny bump of crystal and that's a mess. Now that crystal's hitting New York, I always say they might call her tina over here but she's still not coming near me. But tonight I do the bump of crystal and then I can feel the k hitting or is it the acid, and then the woman says I'm Naomi and we go over to the sinks to look in the mirror. We go back onto the dance floor and I'm high but not euphoric and I'm looking at the lights to bring everything up.

I can't really dance because pretty soon everything's fighting it out in my head, and Stephen and Naomi and I keep going back to the bathroom. I've still got my backpack with me and I pull out this aromatherapy oil blend called Energize and I'm passing it around the bathroom and everyone's loving it. This guy Hector hands me his card and says come to my place afterwards and Naomi and Stephen and I are studying the design on the card and looking at our eyes in the mirror and smelling Energize. The woman who gives out paper towels is smiling at us and I offer her the oil but she says no thank you honey and I wonder if she thinks it's poppers.

Then Naomi and I go out to the dance floor and Naomi's smiling and I'm trying to smile but feeling like my head's filled with cotton then gelatin then those rubber balls you get in the machine for twenty-five cents. We do some more k and then the club is closing and we're looking around for Stephen who's supposed to give us a ride. Stephen runs up to us and we go outside and it's absolutely freezing but light out already, I can't believe it. We walk to Stephen's car, he's got a black Mercedes and Naomi and I give each other looks like is this really happening?

We start driving and I relax, listening to the music and watching the buildings move by. The streets are empty and the sun's all bright and the music's loud and everything's okay. We get to the apartment and Hector isn't there, so we go to the convenience store and Ultra Naté is singing about going insane, which is way too obvious, but sometimes that's how it is. Naomi and I start dancing in the back and Stephen's looking for something. I get a gallon of water and we go to Hector's apartment and this time he answers.

We go up and it's one of those k-holes on the stairs, only not so severe because of the rest of the drugs. It's six flights up, though, and by the time we get there I'm fading. We walk in and I sit down on the sofa and I'm stuck but I have to go to the bathroom. I get to the bathroom and the acid starts hitting hard. I can see the tree branches climbing in the window; I'm peering out into the air shaft to see who's there, waiting for someone to look in at me, but it's just me and the trees. I sit down on the toilet to piss and I feel like I'm giving birth. That's an acid moment if I've ever had one.

Then I go back into the room and Hector is passing around this one-bump-at-a-time vial of k. I do a tiny bump and whoops I'm somewhere else. Everything is kind of vibrating and the music's louder and someone's cutting lines of coke and I don't want any more coke but I do some anyway. Stephen, Naomi, and I are on the sofa. Then there's this woman Loli cutting coke with I guess her boyfriend, who reminds me of this guy Kevin who used to deal in Boston because he's got that vacantly focused and confused look on his face. Plus, he's wearing a vest with no shirt and he's all sweaty and hairy like Kevin.

Then there's Teddy who's probably Hector's boyfriend. And that's all. I go to the bathroom again. I'm drinking glass after glass of water but I still feel dehydrated and every ten minutes I have to piss. Loli looks me in the eyes and says this is amazing, it was so magical when we met at the club. This only happens once in a while. I'm thinking wait until you crash, but I just smile.

Hector brings out some nose drops and he won't tell anyone what's in them. He says just use one or two drops and then sniff. It feels like liquid e because all the sudden I've got that *hello* and I get up and start dancing. But then my body hurts too much so I sit down again. Hector's passing around purified sea water—I swear—I take a teaspoonful and it tastes so salty I want to vomit but it does kind of clear things up.

Three other guys arrive and they're coked out of their minds, pacing around the room and the room's not big. Naomi and I keep exchanging looks like what's going on?, and then Hector starts reading from some new-agey techno book, and when I come back from the bathroom, Naomi's talking about how she used to live across the street until her apartment building burned down. She woke up surrounded by flames, but got out with her drugs and her money so it wasn't that bad.

I can't tell if Naomi's lying but Hector says it was a sign. Hector's trying to have a spiritual connection with everyone, so he keeps looking Naomi in the eyes and saying *you were saved for a reason*. Then Hector asks me what I do and I can't even talk so I just smile. It's 9 a.m. and I want to go home and crawl into bed, but I don't want to get there before noon because then Jon might be there and he's never done drugs, so I don't know how I would explain.

At this point I'm having a nervous breakdown but I don't want to show it. I want to call someone up and say HELP ME, but there's no one in New York I can feel that vulnerable with. I think of calling Andee in Montana, but he'd freak out about me doing drugs. Mostly I just want to lie down in the bathtub, but I don't want to leave Naomi alone in the living room because Hector's getting kind of creepy and the nose drops are gone.

Hector and Loli realize they're from the same neighborhood in Colombia, that they know the same people in the Cali Cartel or maybe this is just a k-paranoia moment or more like an acid, e, k, coke, crystal shoot-out. Someone brings out some pot and that calms me, but now my throat's even more dried-out. Stephen says bye, he needs to go to business school in an hour and we're all confused. I go to the bathroom again and the air's better, I just want to go into the air shaft and cry but I don't know how to get there. I'm thinking maybe I need this world of drugs because I don't have anything else.

I take out my contacts because I'm afraid they're going to stick to my eyes and when I come out of the bathroom I can't see anything and the music's all soft or maybe I can't hear anything either. I want to scream HELP but instead I just collapse on the sofa next to Naomi and look at my pager: 10:30. Naomi's got some German science magazine and inside there's an ad that says Ketamin, which is what k is. In the ad, there's a computer-generated person with one eye in three dimensions and the other eye inside a triangle. It's an advertisement for a k-hole. Hector says does anyone here read German and I can't believe what I'm seeing, I keep saying is this *real*?

Hector starts flaking out about the meaning of all of us being there together and the way we learn from sharing what we know and one of the cokeheads starts laughing and says that's fucking bullshit and they go into the other room. Finally it's 11:30, and Naomi and I decide to leave. She lives in Williamsburg too and I'm grateful because we can share a cab and I'll actually get home.

We get outside and the sun is so bright I have to squint and there's all this dust on the street or is that snowflakes and I can't tell which cars are going which way. Naomi flags down a cab. We get inside and I feel like we're driving through a tunnel but it's just the street. I tell Naomi I'm on acid too and her eyes widen and she says oh. We get on the bridge and I'm sure we're on the wrong bridge but Naomi says it's definitely right. Then we get onto Broadway in Williamsburg where the JMZ train is elevated over the street and it looks like night outside.

I've still got a half-vial of k in my pocket, but

I don't ever want to do another bump of anything in my life. I want to sleep for at least twenty-four hours though I'm worried I'll just lie in bed wired. I'm thinking what should I do with the k, should I throw it away or should I give it to Naomi. We get to my house and we exchange numbers, I give Naomi a kiss and then I say wait, press the vial into her hand. She looks at the vial and her eyes light up and I know it was the right thing to do.

I get into my apartment and immediately I feel more relaxed. My apartment's so dark and sometimes that feels bleak but today it just feels like so much calm. I strip off my clothes and run into the shower. The shower gets me horny, I start flexing my muscles and opening the shower curtain so I can watch myself jerking off in the mirror. I smack my tits until they pop up and get red, lick my armpits and grab my ass and stand away from the water stream so I can smell my sweat.

I'm wired and I need to come, but I don't want to do it alone. I get out of the shower and call a phone sex line, talk to some guy who wants to suck my dick and doesn't mind driving over, so I figure I can't turn down the opportunity. No one ever wants to come to Williamsburg. I put on sweatpants and a tank-top and I'm looking all butch. I really want to get fucked because drugs make my asshole relaxed and then getting fucked doesn't hurt. I'm hoping the guy's hot but I'm not expecting anything, since the first thing he said was do you like older guys, and then, I just want to service you.

I'm fantasizing anyway. I'm all wired, thinking I'm never going to sleep, and grabbing my dick to stay a little hard and pacing around the room, looking out the windows and then shutting the curtains because it's way too bright. Then the phone rings and the guy's downstairs. I let him in and he's this short, skinny middle-aged guy with a potbelly and a Yankees cap. I sit down on the sofa and he gets on his knees to suck my dick. I put his hands on my chest and I caress the back of his head and I'm hard.

Then I stand up and start fucking the guy's face and he moans but then pulls away to do poppers. Then he takes my dick all the way in his mouth but starts gagging so he takes a break and says am I doing okay? I say yeah, feels great — and it does feel great but already I realize that after I come I won't feel so good. I sit down and he goes back to sucking my dick and this time he's deep-throating and I pull my shirt up and he grabs my tits and then I stand up and grab the back of his head and push my dick all the way into his throat.

I start pumping and grabbing onto the guy's head and then I'm groaning and I can feel myself getting close and then my dick starts spasming and the guy's moaning and I'm gasping and I pull my dick out and then I shoot right between his eyes. He reaches up to rub my come into his hair. He says I'd love to do this again but I say I think it was a one-time thing, thanks. He walks out the door with a thin coating of come that spreads from the bridge of his nose, but I'm too wired to think it's funny, looking through all my jars of vitamins for some kind of tranquilizer. I used to have Valium for emergencies, but now the closest thing I can find is a melatonin. I take one, get undressed, and believe it or not the melatonin works.

Our Relationship

We're in line at the post office, this woman turns to me and says is that a moving notice? I'm moving, but not yet. This is Express Mail.

She says has anyone ever told you you're wearing my sweater from 1952 and I laugh, someone else grins. We hold hands. Then she says the line's moving very fast. It is.

She wants to know how you can tell if a cd works. The Who, she saw them here in 1962. Turandot, unless that's a coffee cake. There are no cds in the cases: that's how it works.

Hypoglycemia

The train gets to Penn Station and I'm hoping my trick's hot because I'm horny as hell so I wouldn't mind getting off. I'm meeting him at his office nearby. On my way there, a bunch of people are selling counterfeit train tickets and there's a guy with a bullhorn saying DON'T PURCHASE TICKETS OUTSIDE. I get to the building and go upstairs to buzz the trick. Turns out he's this aging hippy with stringy hair and a scruffy face. I smile and say nice to meet you.

We go into the office and he lays some sheets down over the rug. I say what would you like to do, and he walks over and starts kissing me, but his breath tastes like pot and rotten cheese, so I lean my head to the side and run my hands up and down his back while he kisses my neck and starts to unbutton my shirt. We take off our clothes and then I lie down on the sheet, he lies down next to me and puts his arms around me. He kisses my neck and I kiss his shoulder and move my hands all over his thighs. He grabs my dick, then leans over me and licks one of my tits, down my chest. I put his hands on my chest so I'll stay turned on.

He moves his lips around my dick and I'm hard and he's licking the shaft of my dick and over my balls and he's grabbing my tits. I move his hands to my armpits and he keeps licking the shaft of my dick and I put my hand on the back of his neck. I want to say *take it in your mouth*, but I don't know if he's into that sort of talk, so I just moan every time he gets close to my cockhead, hoping that he'll get the hint.

I'm glad the blinds aren't drawn, because I

like to have a view when I'm getting my cock sucked and my attention starts to drift. In this case, I'm looking out at a wall of windows, and there are infinite possibilities for people to eavesdrop. I picture every possible cliché — the bored office drone, hard-on in slacks; the horny construction worker, overalls pulled down for access; the salivating old man, fantasizing about a piece of me. All I see is a woman in a mauve suit, and it does look like she's got her eyes on me. Funny.

Then the trick stops sucking and lies down next to me so I get on top of him and start licking one of his tits, down his grey-haired flabby chest, to his dick. I take his whole dick right into my mouth and then suck slowly up and down. He puts a hand on the back of my neck and that gets me going, I start sucking fast and then slow and then fast, pulling on his cockhead and then tightening my lips around the shaft. I can tell he's going to come, so I start jerking him off and sucking the cockhead, then just jerking, but he keeps stopping me from getting him off so I jerk more slowly, like I'm not in a hurry at all.

He grabs onto one of my hands and I pull on one of his tits with my other hand and go back to sucking his dick. Then I move my hand down and start jerking slowly with his dick still in my mouth. He starts moaning like a seagull and I move my mouth off his dick and he squeezes my hand and says *slowly*. I jerk his dick slowly but firm and he starts cawing again and then he comes. I lay down next to him and play with his balls, he says oh that was so sweet.

We get dressed and he says I have these two friends coming up from DC, one of them's my age and one of them's your age, and I'm wondering how much you'd charge for about two hours with all of us. I say three hundred, three-fifty. I don't want to make it too high because he might be a regular. He says great, they'll be down in a few weeks and I'll give you a call—but I'll call you again before then too. I don't want them to know that I'm paying you, though. Let's just say we met at a bar on Christopher Street. I'm thinking the other guy my age is probably a whore too and we'll both be pretending we're not; that ought to be fun.

I kiss him goodbye and then I go downstairs and realize I need to eat right away. I stop at a corner store and get one of those whole wheat rolls with the walnuts in them, then walk towards Zen Palate because that's the closest place where I can eat, even though I'm sick of it. Then I remember Zen Palate doesn't have a bathroom except in the fancy part, so I stop at the Virgin Megastore to piss, notice that they're playing the Spice Girls movie in Times Square. Talk about depressing. Of course I get distracted by the listening stations at Virgin, and then I'm hypoglycemic and I can't stop staring at this enormous picture of Celine Dion, thinking *what's going on?* Finally I get a grip and get outside, buy some almonds and I'm walking along Eighth Avenue all wired and disoriented and I can't find Zen Palate. I call them and it's on Ninth.

I eat and then I crash, it's nightime and I'm in Manhattan and I don't know what to do. I read a story about a guy who's a high-class whore in Hong Kong; the story's dull. I don't want to go home because I feel too sad and exhausted, not really horny but craving some sort of temporary intimacy. I figure I'll walk over to the East Side Club because I'm sick of the Chelsea boys at the West Side Club. I don't have a clue who goes to the East Side Club, but I'm curious. Though it'll probably just be East Side yuppies and tourists from the Midtown hotels.

I'm walking over to the East Side and then I realize I'm hungry again, so I stop in this pastry shop with big glass windows that has a grilled vegetable and tofu sandwich. They microwave the sandwich but it tastes okay. It's just me and the two guys who work there, so I watch the people at Sbarro across the street while I'm eating. Then these five guys come in and they're just standing in the doorway singing reggae songs or something in this staccatto, threatening way. I can tell something's going to happen, I'm thinking maybe the store's going to be robbed so I'll just pretend I don't notice. I'm kind of scared but mostly just frozen.

Then all the sudden there are pastries flying around the room, and at first I think they're being thrown at the guys who work there, then bouncing off the wall in front of me. Then pastries start hitting my jacket, a scone pounds me in the face and explodes onto the wall. Then a few more break apart against the wall and then the guys leave.

I've got pastries all over me and my food and the guy behind the counter comes over and says sorry, I'm sorry, I'll make you another sandwich. I say don't worry about it. I go into the bathroom to breathe, realize I'm kind of shaken. I don't know what just happened, I guess it was some sort of bashing, even though today I'm dressed all normal for my tricks and I don't know whether I look like that much of a fag. Maybe I just look like a different kind of fag. Or maybe the guys were drugged out and throwing pastries at the whiteboy seemed like the right thing to do.

I feel like when I did that porn video and all they said beforehand was will you be a bottom? Got there and before I knew it there was spray paint all over my shirt, a hood over my head and a collar around my neck. Got dragged through gravel and then they wanted to make me eat dog food. That's the only time I said *blue*, which was the code word for too much. I said I'm *vegan*. Then we went back to business. When I left, I felt like suddenly the world was different and slow.

Now I'm exhausted but I walk over to the East Side Club anyway, get there and I decide to wait outside for a few minutes to see who's going in. I wait about fifteen minutes and only two guys go in; they're pretty frightening. So I walk over to catch the train. I get on the F and figure I can transfer to the J and go home or get off at Fourteenth Street and see what happens. I decide to go home—I'm completely drained—but then I get off at Fourteenth Street. As I'm walking out, I link eyes with this guy who's kinda hot. Then I turn around and he turns around too. Then we both turn around a third time and I smile and motion him over.

I wait on the steps for him to follow me outside. I can't very well follow him onto his train, I mean I could but it seems easier for him to follow me out. He walks up the stairs and stands right next to me. He says what's up. I say I'm just bored and horny, how about you. He doesn't say anything. I say you want to walk over to Union Square? He says how far is that? I say two blocks that way and I point. It's a beautiful night. He says okay.

We walk along and exchange names and what train we were taking and he asks what do you do for a life instead of what do you do, which I think is nice. His name's Joe and he's an actor. We walk to Union Square and then we end up talking about plays, he's interesting enough and it's still warm outside. I say do you want to make out, and he looks around, I say not here? I keep looking him in the eyes but I can't tell what he wants and then he finally puts a hand on my pants and I put a hand on his pants. He's moving around to find my dick and his is already hard. I move closer.

He's looking around; I mean, it's true that Union Square is brightly lit and there are cops all over, but no one really stays in the park, they just walk through. He says have you met people here before, and I tell him a story about this guy I met. It was raining that night but I was too lonely to care, sitting in the park because I couldn't think of anywhere else to go and it was kind of warm. This guy walked up and we smoked the rest of his joint and talked for a while—it was kind of romantic. He asked me if I wanted to go over to the peepshows on Third Avenue, we went into a booth and I started kissing his neck and then he opened the door and left.

I don't tell Joe the part about kissing the other guy on the neck because I can't figure out whether Joe's straight. Joe says what're you into? I say I love to suck dick and I love to make out. Joe says he likes to get fucked, I say I'd like to fuck you some time. Joe starts to slide his hand into my pants and my dick's getting hard now and I'm grabbing Joe's dick, but then someone walks toward us so we both sit up. Then all's clear so I unbutton my pants. Joe grabs my dick and immediately I'm hard. I'm trying to pull his dick out but he isn't exactly helping me.

Someone else walks toward us and I throw

my coat over my dick and kind of laugh, keep jerking off. Joe moves away from me a little until the person passes, but then he moves back next to me. I unzip his pants and take out his dick. Joe's grabbing my dick really hard and staring at it and then looking around us, back and forth. I say do you want to go to Stuyvesant Park, it's darker there. He says where's that? I say two blocks that way. He says what time is it. Midnight.

Stuyvesant Park is too crowded for Joe, and we can't find anywhere else that's even half-private. We're walking around and I'm hoping this isn't going to end up in nothing. Finally Joe brings me to this park in between two tall modern buildings, he says how does this look? I say perfect. There's a circular concrete bench that's kind of in the dark and you can see anyone coming long before they arrive. Sure, the people in the buildings have a prime view, but who cares — as long as there aren't any cops involved.

So we sit down and right away he says can I suck your dick? Then he unbuttons my pants and bends over and sucks. I put my hand on the base of his neck, he's doing okay but he can't take much of my dick in his mouth. Someone walks toward us, so Joe sits up and I put my coat over my hard-on and grab Joe's thigh. The guy passes, I say my turn and I unzip Joe's pants, bend over and take his dick in my mouth. I taste his precome right away; I love the sweetness. I'm sucking fast because I want him to come in my mouth, but then he says quick get up so I sit up and he zips his pants.

There's this guy running towards us with his dog, but then he turns around so I relax though Joe's still tense. Then the guy comes running back, and running all around but not really looking at us, I say why don't we jerk off? Joe says I don't know, I'm grabbing my dick under my coat and I hold the coat up so Joe can see my dick. He says you've got a nice dick. I say thanks, he says how big is it? I say bigger than a baseball bat, but Joe doesn't laugh.

The guy with the dog is still running around, and then he walks over and sits about as close as he can to us without leaving the grass. I say looks like he wants to watch. We sit for a while and the guy's still there, pretending he's not looking. At first I thought he was a fag, but now I figure he must be straight because otherwise he'd either stare or come over or at least say something. Or get away. Instead he's sitting there smoking a cigarette and pretending he's not looking at us.

Then the guy smokes another cigarette. And then another. I want to say bitch go home, but I don't think Joe would be into that. I want to grab Joe's dick, but he's too nervous. Joe says what time is it, I say 12:45, he says maybe we should go. I say let's just wait another few minutes.

Finally the guy leaves, I say you wanna get off now? Joe takes out his dick and says tell me about fucking me again. I take out my dick and we're both hard. I'm getting into the talk, Joe says are you close, I say I can come anytime. He says do you shoot far. I say it kind of depends, sometimes I do and sometimes I don't. He says I love it when a guy shoots far. I've got my hand on his thigh and he's got his hand under my balls. He says I think I'm ready and I look over at him, I know I've got that look in my eyes when there's nothing there but sex. I jerk my dick and I stand up a bit and try to clench my asshole because I think that helps me shoot.

Some of my come shoots about a foot or two

and the rest gets on my fingers, I figure that's a pretty good show. I lick the come off my fingers and Joe starts zipping up his pants. He says I don't think I can come. I say are you sure? He says yeah, it's really late. I say you're just going to be up longer when you get home. He says yeah, but I don't think I can come here. I say okay, button my pants and put on my coat.

We walk to the subway and Joe's kind of quiet. I say I'll give you my number and you can come over and I'll fuck you sometime. We get to the subway. I say you want to give me yours? He says I can't—I live with two guys and they're straight. All the sudden Joe looks worn-out.

Four Hugs

Four Hugs

This trick sounds like the same flake I got two weeks ago, the one who called me at 3 a.m. and then didn't even bother to answer the door when I arrived. The guy tonight has a different phone number and address, but something about his voice sounds the same. They always say trust your intuition, it's always right, but I've learned that's not really true so I head out in a cab.

I get to the trick's apartment and he lives in the building on Avenue A that must be the ugliest thing in the East Village, this brick building from the '60s with huge concrete balconies. They were renovating it last year and I couldn't understand why they didn't just tear it down. I look inside and it's kind of posh.

The guy buzzes me in and I go upstairs, his door's got a police lock in the center—I'm in a paranoid mood, hoping the extra lock isn't there to keep the neighbors or the cops away from the stench of rotting flesh on the other side. He opens the door and he's studying me with this scowl on his face, I guess another whore might have a pose to go with that scowl but I've got nothing. He's tall, too—for a second I think am I really six feet?

He offers me a drink and I ask for water; his apartment's beautiful. I say from outside, I never would have expected the apartment would look like this. It's a two-story loft—sleek and modern and spare in that Europe-meets-Japan kind of way. Dining-room table that looks like it's ready for a conference and a black-leather sofa with—is that really a fur?—on it. Gross.

We go into the bedroom and he says is this

okay. I say sure. He says I'd like a massage first, so I get lotion out of my bag. Still can't tell if he likes me. There's a futon on the floor and everything in the room is on the floor too, only there's not much in the room. I wonder about rich people who don't have anything laying around: where do they keep it all? The radio's tuned to the BBC; they're talking about the bombing of Kosovo, and the trick says this ought to relax me.

I start to unlace my boots and he pulls off his clothes and says which way should I lie on the bed? I say you choose; he's obviously tense. I take off my clothes and I straddle him, start to rub lotion into his back. He says I like it deep, so I push hard and it's nice feeling his skin, being on top of him. I get into the massage, letting my tension leave my body as I push into him. I try to get aroused, but my dick doesn't budge. I push into his body with my elbows, forearms, and then wrap my hands under his chest to his armpits, and suddenly I'm hard, grabbing him under his armpits and up to his shoulders, feeling his sweat on my fingers.

I move to his ass and then down his legs to his feet. Rubbing his feet against my chest, I'm turned on and then he flips over, picks up the remote control to change the radio to music. He says that was great, and starts sucking on my chin. I get on top of him and suck on his neck, he puts his arms around me, then picks them up and replaces them, over and over, hugging me from different directions. I relax, lie in his arms and then lick down his neck to his nipples, to his crotch, to his dick.

His dick is big and it curves upward, I'm nervous about getting fucked but excited about sucking. I start with the cockhead and then move slowly down and then back and forth until my throat relaxes and his dick pushes back. He puts his hands on my neck and pets me gently, moaning, and I'm sucking up and down, hoping he'll suddenly get close to coming and I can jerk him off. I suck for a while and he's shaking, but I can tell he's not going to come, so I move up to kiss him on the lips, lying on top of him.

He flips me onto my back and then he's on top of me, my legs in the air and his dick right at my asshole. I'm thinking this is definitely not the way I want to get fucked, but I figure I'll let him tease my asshole for a while then we can change positions, put a condom on, and go from there. I pull his hands to my chest, then lean my neck up to take his dick in my mouth and he grabs my head, fucks my face for a minute, and then I relax onto the bed.

His dick pushes against my asshole, I can feel the heat of pain going through my body and I'm thinking it's going to hurt too much to get fucked, and then his dick inches into my asshole and slides gently all the way inside. I know I should sit up and pull myself away but I don't, he's fucking me and it's so easy without a condom. He says this is so beautiful, and it does feel amazing, though I'm thinking about which emergency safer sex workshop I have to go to — is there one for whores who let their tricks fuck them without a condom because it doesn't hurt as much?

He's fucking me and he says *it's so beautiful* again and I kind of want to cry, and I want to say don't come inside me but I can't even say that, I don't know why. I can't believe he's fucking me with his whole dick in my ass and it's so easy, I'm so hard for him and I'm not touching myself at all. I can feel

175

myself getting close to coming, I'm moaning and then I shoot all over my chest. I've never come like that before — without someone touching me — I ease myself off his dick and I'm lying on my back wondering what I'm feeling, the rush and the crash.

He asks me to turn over, so I'm on my stomach and he gets on top of me; he's one of those guys who needs to at least pretend he's fucking in order to come. His dick's right up against my asshole, and I reach back to help him get off, but really I'm covering myself. I'm worried some of his come might get in my asshole, even though I realize that's kind of ridiculous, considering his whole dick was just in there. He starts moaning like he's crying, and then I can't tell if he's coming but I figure that's what happened because he lies down next to me and puts his arms around me.

The radio's playing some old song and I struggle to catch the words, something about not just being another one-night lady. It's always funny like that. I'm looking at the black pillows, white sheets, and the room in tones of grey, flickering in candlelight, looking out the window at the building across the street and everything's so still. I'm filled with a sad sense of paralysis but there's comfort there too, I'm letting my body release all of its pain instead of pretending everything's casual. Me and this guy are lying there together and it's like we're one body until I move slightly to reach for some water, and he says do you need to use the bathroom?

I go to the bathroom and it's all black and white — stark — and I look at my chest in the mirror and there's dried come all over me, how'd that get there? Oh right, I came on myself. I look in the shower and there's Japanese shampoo, the only thing in the room except Japanese liquid soap. I think it's funny the way everything is so blank on purpose. I wash up and then go back into the bedroom.

It's dark in the bedroom and he says are you okay? I almost want to answer him, but I say yeah. The whole room smells like come, and he's sitting on the bed with his laptop. He's put my clothes in a pile and I get dressed, follow him into the living room, and he goes into another room—filled with computers and stacks of videos—there's his stuff. I notice a spiral staircase that leads to another room, I guess. He gives me the money and we kiss goodbye, this feels too monumental.

I get to the street and I'm thinking about something I heard on the radio, how everyone needs at least four hugs a day, and I'm wondering if that trick counted as four hugs. I get to the store, and there's the guy I usually give money to, slumped over; he says I only slept three hours last night. I'm choosing vegetables, and someone's screaming *Pancho Villa*, Pancho Villa. I turn around and there's this guy in a huge Mexican hat, grinning at me in that way drunk straight guys do when they want sex. He says I like your jacket and I say thanks, laughing; I go back to choosing vegetables, and someone walks by with a dog. The guy screaming Pancho Villa says I like dogs—with a little garlic, some chiles, and jalapeño—and I turn to go into the store.

The Factory

Ron has a painting of a Georgia O'Keefe quote that says, "I hate flowers. I just paint them because they're cheaper than models," which I think is funny. He says are we going to have to sit and talk or can we just get down to business? I say business sounds fine, so we go into the bedroom and get undressed. He starts touching me really soft, which always makes me tense. I want to slap him, so I move down where he can't reach me and start sucking his dick. I'm sucking and sucking, thinking when is he going to come but acting like I'm savoring every second. He's petting my face like we're in love. After he comes, he says lie down next to me, which is always a sign that I'm going to have to stay.

Ron looks me in the eyes and says who is your favorite author? I say David Wojnarowicz, and Ron gets this glazed look in his face like his ecstasy is kicking in and he says I knew David, he would have loved to hear that. Ron starts stroking my arm and looking me in the eyes and he says you know, you kind of look a little like David. I saw David just before he died, someone from the Museum of Modern Art came to his apartment and wanted to make a deal for three paintings. David said he wasn't going to make any deals.

Ron caresses my arm and tells me about David Wojnarowicz while I stare at the etching on the wall, which looks familiar but I can't quite place it. Turns out it's a Jasper Johns, Ron says this is my shrine to Jasper. I ask Ron if he built the walls and he says he built everything, which probably means he had everything built. But it is beautiful: floor-to-ceiling shelves and recessed lighting, built-in tables and dressers. Listening to Ron talk about all these famous gay artists, I feel like I've entered into history.

Then Ron shows me his own art and I stare at the way the light pours through the geometry of shapes and the layers of paint with delicate designs at the center. I want to ask Ron if he's heard of Rose Stern. I feel so relaxed, like something magical is happening. I don't mean magical in some new-agey way, just beautiful and calming like a deep part of me is suddenly awake and I'm not sure how.

When I leave, it's like I'm in the world where I've always wanted to be. Looking into the store windows in Soho like each one is a different abandoned universe. I mean, Soho's gross during the day, but at 2 a.m. it's empty and iridescent. I get another page, but the guy's already called someone else. He says you were the first one I called; if this guy doesn't work out, I'll give him the money and then call you back.

So I figure I'll stay in Manhattan for a little while. I go over to Veselka and get lentil soup and it's delicious, all my senses feel activated. Watching the people like I'm watching a painting. I still feel energetic and vaguely horny, like I wouldn't mind sucking cock and getting off, and when will I ever be right down the street from the Bijou on a Saturday night? So I go over there.

I get there and it's insane, so crowded that there aren't any empty lockers. I have to walk around with my coat and backpack. As usual, everyone's just moving in circles. The walls are lined with guys waiting for a cubicle to open up. Everyone has this awful vacant look like they're being hunted: I swear.

No one will even look each other in the eyes. I see a couple just touching each other—I mean, not even groping or anything — and every time someone looks at them, they stop. Everyone just keeps walking around. Then there are guys hired to be monitors, walking around with flashlights. I see two guys groping each other *through their pants*, and a monitor goes over to them and says you can't do that here.

I go back to the bathroom and stand by the urinals, jerking off. Guys look at me and then see someone else watching and leave. It's ridiculous. Finally this guy stands next to me and pulls out his dick, grabs my dick and I grab his. Then another guy comes over and starts jerking off with us. It's hot but they're so frenzied. They come in about two minutes and I just stand there jerking off and smiling. One guy grabs my balls and the other guy puts his hand on my chest and I come, lick the come off my fingers. They laugh.

Then I sit by the entrance and watch people. One of the guys I had sex with comes over and I say what is this they're showing on that screen, we can't do that in here, and he laughs, but everyone else pretends they don't hear anything. I start pointing, saying what's going on? What's going on? WHATEVER HAPPENED TO RESISTANCE? The guy I'm sitting with tries to convince me to go home with him for a second round, but I'm not into it.

I leave — and I'm disturbed but still so energetic. It's like I can feel the contrast between everyone else's fear and my comfort, so I feel calm. I think well I might as well go to the Boiler Room for the last few minutes. Get there and they're playing an okay house song, I say what's going on? I'm laughing and staring like I'm on e, saying what's going on in here? I'm *wired*, take off my coat and do a little runway. This guy looks like he's in shock, I lean over to him and say don't be scared, honey. There's a guy with his shirt pulled up like he's on the Skins team, stumbling around like he might fall over any minute. I say when did they get a go-go dancer?

Then I start going up to just about everyone in the bar and saying the most random things. Whenever someone cruises me, I make faces at him. Two boys say you look like trouble, let's go out and make trouble. I find a scarf on the floor and ask every single guy in the bar if it's his, then put it around my neck and say thank you for coming to the Factory, thank you everyone, thank you.

The Gym

Usually the music's okay — or at least bearable — but today they're playing the absolute worst shit that I've ever heard in my life. It's a compilation of airy mid-eighties pop songs with dance beats. It's not even bad songs that were hits; it's bad songs that didn't make it. The only song I recognize is some Debbie Gibson thing — or maybe it's Tiffany — I don't know. How the hell am I supposed to work out to this shit?

I'm looking around for someone to talk to, but no one here talks to me. I don't want a career and I don't live in Chelsea and I don't go to the Pines. No one seems to notice how horrible the music is. Finally I spot Douglas — I gave him a blow job in the sauna once, but he says hi to me anyway. I say you're not wearing your headphones — and the music is at an all-time low. I go back to working out, but I just can't stop laughing. Guys are looking at me like what's she on? I've got my hands over my ears and I'm trying to stop laughing.

I get back to working out. I figure I'll pull against the music, like if I do enough reps it will stop. I'm doing cable rows and staring out the window and it starts to pour outside, and then it's hailing and people in the gym stop to stare outside, instead of the usual people staring in. I'm watching the people on the street running in shock, the few with umbrellas, the few who don't seem to care. I can't stop staring at the hail, somehow I feel like it's coming out of me and I'm just watching it pound the sidewalk. I can feel my eyes kind of bugging out and then this calm washes into my head and down my body. Then the hail turns back to rain and I go back to working out.

Provincetown

I'm on the beach, the guys next to me start talking about a program in New York that pays a drug-addicted pregnant woman two hundred dollars to have an abortion. I lean over and say actually it's for Norplant, the guy says wait maybe it's tubal ligation. I'm about to say whatever happened to treatment, but the guy says I think it's a great idea.

I guess I'm not shocked, but my arguments aren't as clear as I want them to be. This guy's a doctor in New Orleans, he says something about drug-addicted mothers with fifteen children and four-year-olds running wild on the streets. I think about how pointless political discussions are, but still I want to offer an opinion that might turn on lightbulbs.

It's getting tense, so I say there's our beach discussion, and we all laugh. The sun starts to go down and there's a breeze like three clichés put together: smelling like the sea, a warm embrace gently massages me—it even rhymes. The water is ice, but queers come from all over the world to bake here. Some couples hold hands for the first time in public, you can see it in their eyes: the dunes stretching on and on.

All the sudden the sun's gone and it's chilly, everyone starts packing up. I put on my bathing suit, grab my backpack, and I'm over the big hill by the water, looking down over the vast expanse of dunes. On the way, it was desert, but now the tide's come in and it's lush fields of grass and lakes and streams, a startling world that makes me breathe deeper.

And everywhere there are fags trudging through the tidal pools: splash, plop, splash. It's this mass exodus of explorers with backpacks and sun umbrellas, fields and streams filling with little boys hiking through the sand.

The Tide

It's 1 a.m, which is when all the bars close in Provincetown, so I figure I better get up the hill and over to the action. I hurry to Commercial Street, rush to the bay and sure enough there's a group of guys waiting around. But that's all they're doing. So I start grabbing my dick through my pants, and then I take it out, and pretty soon someone's on his knees against the fence, sucking me.

Then suddenly there are guys surrounding us — all jerking off — I don't know where everyone came from. One guy in a Stüssy hat keeps looking at my earrings, either he's into them or — I don't know. His eyes are bulging and I think he's kind of freaked out. He's one of the only other young guys around and I pull him behind me. He's grabbing my ass but not low enough and the other guy's still sucking my dick, I lean over to kiss his head and then I pull my dick away because I'm about to come.

The Stüssy guy steps back to watch me jerking off and the guy who was sucking my dick moves over to someone else, so I bend over to suck another guy's dick, cockhead that expands in my throat. I lean up and some older guy holds his poppers to my nose — yuck, I push his hand away but smile. The guy sucking moves on to a third guy; I'm feeling a bit neglected, but not enough to let the other guy on his knees keep sucking me — his mouth feels so dry it hurts.

The poppers guy is holding the poppers down for the first guy sucking and that guy pushes them away too. I put my fingers in his ears while he sucks yet another guy's dick — he's got the stamina. Someone tries to rim me but I'm not into it. I turn around to say no thanks but he keeps going so I push his head away. I want to get fucked—I've got condoms and lube and my ass is out, in New York there'd be someone trying to get inside me within seconds.

I take off my shirt and hang it on the fence. I'm jerking off but I'm not really into it. The crowd smells like stale sweat and poppers and then there's the rotten-fish smell from the water. I lean over to suck some guy's huge dick; he's fucking my face hard and I'm taking it, he's grunting but then he pulls away and the first sucker goes for him. I stand up to someone rubbing my chest, his hard dick pressing against my ass. I move his dick to my asshole.

I've got one hand on the sucker's neck and with my other hand I grab the other guy's ass while he's getting sucked. He's moaning and I kiss his neck, then he pulls away and I feel the guy behind me as his dick slides into my ass and he gasps, lips at my neck, hands grabbing my thighs. The sucker's taking a break, cupping my balls and I'm jerking off and the other guy's got his dick all the way in my ass.

I reach down to my pants and take out a condom, look up and wow everyone's gathered against the fence watching me. I feel like a safer-sex harm reduction demonstration as I lean over and slide the condom onto the guy's dick, pull out my lube and get him all wet. Then I put his dick against my asshole again and he practically shoves it in, which makes me gasp but I'm relaxed now so it's okay. I'm bent over and he's fucking me, yes, and then the sucker gets underneath me, and wow.

I stand up and the guy's grabbing my chest and fucking me and there's the Stüssy guy right beside me rubbing my tits, and all over there are guys looking at me and jerking off. I feel like I'm putting on a show. I bend my knees and lean over to ask the guy sucking if he wants me to come in his mouth. He nods yes and then I start pumping hard and he's taking it, the guy fucking me is grabbing his head and there it is fuck I'm coming I'm practically screaming and the guy sucking is gagging hard and then I pull away.

Everyone looks like they're in awe. They all start pulling up their pants like they're ready to go, I pull my ass off the guy's dick and turn around to kiss him — he's not bad-looking. Then I lean down to kiss the guy sucking, he says I'm glad I met you. I kiss him again and someone says the tide's coming in. I turn around and sure enough the water's under my boots, two feet further and there will be nowhere to stand.

Fratboy Realness

Every time I go out, I waste an outfit. I'm at the beach, so I don't get dressed during the day. I've got one pair of shorts that I wear all the time, saw them at this weird trance store in the East Village where they don't have much of anything. I thought there's no way in hell I'd ever wear those, but something was drawing me to them. There's a fine line between horribly tacky and absolutely delicious and I like to straddle that line.

Now I love those shorts — they're magenta and teal, 100 percent cotton with lots of pockets; the color of each pocket contrasts with the color of the fabric beneath it. I call them Nepalese raver shorts because they were made in Nepal and I got them at the raver store. I wish I'd bought the blue and orange ones too — I searched every store here for something even slightly interesting, but they all had the same exact shit: knee-length cargo shorts in charcoal, khaki, army green, beige, or — for something a little edgy — orange. In the new plastic fabrics of the moment. Then there are those fucking capri pants in the same goddamned colors. So I wear the Nepalese raver shorts.

When I go to the beach I wear my green swim shorts, but they come off as soon as I get there. For some reason, I put them on when I go to piss in the dunes — or to see what's going on — but otherwise they stay off. I'm trying to lose the tan line. It's quite the fashion parade at the beach, especially since all the tittie queens have arrived. Sarongs are very now, especially on guys who haven't stretched their legs since they started taking steroids. The mini-sarong that stops just above the knee is a sensation. Big straw hats complete the mix-and-match ethnic look. How risqué!

When the tittie queens arrived, I freaked out. It's not that part of me doesn't find some of them hot, but then there's me and I'm scared. I feel like they've invaded my town, even though it's not really my town because I'm only a visitor too. The gay people here were already scary enough—it was already Assimilation Nation—now I don't even know what it is. It's beyond assimilation because these people sure don't look normal.

This town is all about fratboy realness, so I've decided to rate the contestants. Someone came close to a ten last night when he kept pulling up his shorts; he was sporting Teva flip-flops with the fake Guatemalan stitching, plus he kept nodding his head like right-on. Right-on. Right-on. But then I saw his Euro haircut—sorry darling: 8.7. Then there was the boy with a baseball cap on backwards and curly hair that went below the cap in the back. He was wearing khakis cut off unevenly below the knee, I thought he was going to get the award for sure, but when he bent down to adjust his Adidas slip-ons, I saw his underwear: 2xist. Disqualified.

I keep saying that I'm gonna make some money off all of this. I'm going to set up a stand right on the beach—selling steroids and GHB. It gets hot on that beach and the girls need their refreshments. Then I'll hit them with the new drug—Vitamin C— cyanide, honey, 'cause you can't get a better high than that.

That's the other thing—it's such a fucking party town here. I go to the beach around 2, and all the A-listers, B-listers, wannabes and 24-7 lushes (that's most of the fags in this town, especially the tourists) are rushing back to catch the tea dance at the Boatslip. Then the after-tea dance. Then a k-hole, a few bumps to bring you out of it, some fake e to take you higher, crystal so you're up until sunrise, a disco nap, off to the beach, back to tea dance. I don't even know when these girls go to the gym.

If I want to party, I'll party in New York. I came here to get healthy and feel calm, to go jogging somewhere where the air is fresh, to sit on the beach and breathe. And sometimes when I'm walking through the tidal pools, staring through the fields of sea grass to the lighthouse, I get where I want to be, laughing and smiling from deep inside. Or just *feeling* everything, like the other day when someone bent to pick up a mylar balloon in the dunes I almost started crying: someone cares.

I examine each individual grain of sand sparkling in the sun. Fall asleep and wake up to an entirely different color scheme. Watch the tide come in and out. I talk to the bugs because there's no one else to talk to. Yesterday I gave my bug bites names.

I forgot that I need people in my life too. I've started importing friends, but that only works for a few days. The few people here who I like have either gotten married all the sudden, don't go to the beach, or work so much that I never see them. Last night I went out for the first time since the July Fourth weekend started. Jason was visiting, so I felt obligated to show him around a bit.

I guess that means it was the first time I got dressed in a week too. My orange plaid pants with a blue sleeveless tee shirt and blue belt, all my earrings and my bracelets and boots. I even brought out a purse, I was kind of feeling it. We went to the Martin House for dinner because we were gonna splurge, but they'd stopped serving. Then we went to Li'l Deb's for that same veggie burger, which was actually good. Tommi was waiting for a hit of e because she'd just done three the night before. Of course I asked her for k.

Then we walked towards the Vixen, I was ready to go home but Jason wanted to go dancing. For a few minutes I got that party energy from everyone on the street, but then I just wanted cocktails and k, that means time to get away. The Vixen was lesbians from every small town in the country, we were too early for the townies or something. So we turned around, ran into Luis who was waiting for drugs and then Sylvia who was actually fun, working her cinnamon Altoids and her 99-cent Fendi purse. Jason said I'd move here just to hang out with her.

And then we came home and got into bed. I go to bed a lot now. Once at night of course, then in the morning after I get back from jogging, then when I get back from the beach and sometimes after I work out too. Today they were mowing the lawn outside my window at 9 a.m. and that was just what I needed to add to my wonderful calm state.

Tainted Love

Scott, Erica, and I are laughing at all the fashion magazines. We're getting ready to make propaganda and we need some cheesy pictures, but nothing's cheesy enough. I'm complaining that they don't have *Teen People* or wait I don't even see *People*, and where's *Exercise for Men Only*? The woman behind the counter leans over and says *this is not a library*. I say honey I know, we're buying *these* magazines already, and I hold up the stack: *Vogue, Glamour, YM.*

I go back to looking at the magazines. People we know keep coming into the store, this is fun. Andre wants to know what we're doing, the boy with the big teeth who's a barker at — where is he a barker? — anyway he's on break and he's going to the Vault for a cocktail, but I don't want cocktails: I've got propaganda to make. The woman leans over again and says THIS IS NOT A LIBRARY. She's got some European accent that's probably fake, and I'm sure I've heard her say the same thing before, but my adrenaline rush is up, I'm getting annoyed. I say we're looking through the magazines to decide which ones to buy, okay?

My vision's getting blurry from the tension and the boy with the teeth stops momentarily in the door and I swear there's a freeze-frame for a minute and then someone — who is it? — says *we'd rather you leave*. It's all the straight, middle-aged Cape-Cod-for-life women (plus the younger fake European) lined up at the counter like they're uniting against the enemy, and Scott and I are fuming, Erica looks like she's not used to confrontation. I say first I have to spit. Scott says you mean shit. And we're laughing. I say I'll be back with a brick, then I throw the magazines on the shelf and I think the women are laughing too, like we're so disgusting they can't do anything but laugh.

We get outside, what was that about? We don't have a clue. Was it because we were being queeny in a fucking gay resort town? But dammit, now how are we going to make the propaganda? Erica says maybe it's time for a cocktail. Earlier I'd said no cocktails for me but that was earlier, before we got kicked out of the magazine store. I go there several times a week. Erica goes there several times a day. And Scott, who doesn't even live in this town, has been to the magazine store at least ten times this summer.

The point is that Erica's right: it's cocktail time. We slide into The Vault and yes there's the cocktail, but no barker, though there is that boy David from San Francisco and his friends. He says he has a lot of ex-boyfriends so I figure that's what both of his friends are. Then I realize it, he looks exactly like one of my San Francisco roommates' boyfriends from way back. I can't even remember the roommate's name, but the boyfriend was named Randy. David says Randy, that's one of my ex-boyfriends. Wait — now I get it — Randy was my ex-roommate, not my ex-roommate's ex-boyfriend, or boyfriend at the time, but now ex-boyfriend, which I only have one of.

But wait there's a subplot going on. Actually, the conversation with David is the subplot, the plot is that Erica's getting shade from all over the place. She's dressed like a sailor, looks perfect in the leather cruise bar, but right when we get there, the doorman says you can come in, but you've got to move to the front once the bar gets crowded. Like it's some privilege to hang out in this dark dirty dump.

Actually, it is a privilege, because it almost feels like a big-city bar, plus it's the only place in town with porn — and the only place where sex goes on. They're getting around quite a few loopholes.

The management seems to think that Erica's the loophole, though. The bartender repeats what the doorman said, and just when I'm done with my second cocktail — feeling frisky — the bartender comes back to tell us now's the time. To move to the front, that is, smile smile he's telling Erica you know guys *cruise* back there. So there it is: first we get kicked out of the magazine store because I'm a loud queen and then we get kicked out of the leather bar because Erica's a dyke.

Needless to say, when we get out of that bar, we are not loving this town. Erica says this is the worst night of her life, which sounds a bit extreme to me but maybe she hasn't had that many bad nights. We figure we're going to have to go to the straight bars if the gay ones won't have us. Next thing we know, Erica says, we're going to get kicked out of the Vixen because the dykes think Scott's too butch. We go over to the Governor Bradford to check out PJ's karaoke show. This drunk old Cape Codder is doing a jig and reel to some song, just smiling all red-faced like he's never left this bar. PJ spots us right away, puts on that Radiohead song "Freak" — is that what it's called? — anyway it's a good song, I wouldn't know it was Radiohead except it says so on the screen.

PJ does the whole song with her eyes closed, silver eyeliner looking fearless and the wig's all ratty tonight, which is the way I like it. She's got that song down — all emotional and serious — and the crowd doesn't know how to take it. Usually she's just telling them they smell like poop. I scream for her and then two straight guys are doing some gay song like they're camping it up — time to go — blowing PJ kisses we run right out of there.

Look across the street and no way there's Meg-O at the Old Colony — we're really gonna do the straight bars tonight. We go in and Meg-O introduces us to her Irish friends who are loving me; they point a video camera my way and tell me to say something to Ireland. I don't know what to say, but I say something, then I say I need another cocktail, and I'm over to the bar.

The bartender gives me my Stoli-on-the-rocks in a shooter glass, I say what are you doing? She's not amused, but you'd think that in a straight bar that looks like the inside of a rusted oilcan, you'd get strong drinks. I go into the bathroom and it smells like piss from the turn of the century. I bring Erica and Scott back and say this is where the backroom should be, the Vault's got nothing on this place.

We run out after I kiss Meg-O goodbye, she's one of my favorites in this horrible town. Well it's Wednesday so okay we're off to the Vixen. I wasn't gonna go, but now I've had cocktails…so of course I'm going. Sharon's at the door — hello — or is it hello? Anyway we're inside and they're playing fucking "YMCA" — just after I told Scott the music would be okay. Okay, so really it's about the crowd — all the crazy townies and seasonal workers getting smashed and dancing like freaks, that's fun — right?

I get into it, but not for "YMCA." I wouldn't dance to that song if I was on sixteen grams of crystal, four vials of k, and a year's supply of Prozac, Paxil, Zoloft *and* Motrin. But, needless to say, the Motrin dealer's not here so I go to the bar for a drink and there's David, he beat us to the place — told him to go, of course. We're talking and whoops there's Electric Avenue—that's one of the standards that I actually like.

David says no way is he dancing to—I can't remember who sings that song or who he thinks sings that song—but anyway no way is he dancing. I'm dancing, crazy and shaking my ass and soon enough there's four pounds of sweat pouring down my face but then the next song's some unbearable disco monstrosity, I just pretend I'm dancing to Danny Tenaglia late-night at Vinyl. I get centered and then I just go with it, swinging back and forth, shaking my hips and grooving like this is some kind of slow hard house.

Pretty soon our crew is there—Sylvia's grinding against me and her hair is swinging back and forth, Leslie and I are making faces at each other, Erica grabs me and we're fucking—I fucking love the Vixen on a Wednesday, dancing with all the women in the house because the fags are too scared or maybe there's too much or not enough or too much of not enough or just too much not enough—there—with the boys, but then I think why the fuck not? I'm shaking with Christina and I grab some boy over, I have to grab him to get him over and then he gives me some weird sex look—I don't want to sleep with him, just dance. Luckily Sylvia pulls me over—saved by Sylvia.

Dance a little with Scott, hope he doesn't think I'm this crazy because of the liquor because honey I'm this crazy no matter fucking what. Then I remember he knows that. The music's getting worse and worse and Erica brings over another cocktail, then the cocktail's on the bar and I'm bending over for Erica, Sylvia pulls me over and we're getting it on, then shit it's last call.

I go back to the bar, finish my cocktail so I can get another but wait a second it's "Tainted Love," no fucking way I'm SCREAMING and Scott's smiling and Erica's jumping and then I'm flying, singing that song or at least all the words I know. Trying to do runway—running into people who are in the way—and making faces and I get to the back, back to the front, there's Erica and oh no it's over.

Lights are coming on and I'm high from all the sweat, drunk too of course and we're heading out. We say our goodbyes and then we're on our way to Spiritus. I'm singing "Tainted Love" and Erica's stumbling a bit, Scott looks tired. We get to Spiritus and we're yelling as usual, I'm rubbing Erica's head and there's PJ. We take our seats and watch all the action. Erica and I are telling the story of how we got kicked out of the magazine store *and* The Vault.

I'm screaming IT WAS ALL ABOUT TAINTED LOVE and Erica's yelling Mattilda Mattilda, then Sylvia's there too, grinding and we're all singing tainted lo-ove, I want to…run away-ay… duh *dah* dah. Tainted love just saved the night, that's what I say. This cute muscley boy looks back at me and says I want some. I think of following him—he is HOT, ass jumping out of white jeans—but I'm having fun with the Spiritus-until-dawn crowd, so I guess I'm not leaving. Then of course I'm obsessing about it and the guy's gone. Something weird's going on tonight and I'm getting cruised all over, but as usual I don't act on any of it, just keep singing "Tainted Love" because that's what it's all about—I scream FORGET ABOUT ASSIMILATION, IT'S ALL ABOUT TAINTED LOVE.

It's one of those nights, so I go in and buy a

whole vegan pizza. The music inside is better than the music at the Vixen—some '70s funk and I'm shaking it up, no shirt of course after all that sweat. We all squeeze into the photo booth: Erica, PJ, Scott and me—can't decide which background to get, wish they had a real photo booth but oh well just the stickers. Say cheese...

The pictures are scandalous and we're back outside. It's kind of raining and everyone starts to disperse, except for the diehards with umbrellas, and the rest of us just laughing in the street. Spiritus is the best thing about Provincetown. There's Paige, I kiss her hello and she says where's your skirt. I've worn a skirt one time this summer, but Paige is obsessed with it. She's looking extra-fierce tonight—with the blond Afro, tight jeans and a half-shirt, red glitter over her eyes; she's got that realness-with-a-twist thing going on, like I could pass but I'm going to turn it out anyway.

The pizza's ready and by this time it's raining hard out. Erica's disappeared, so Scott, PJ and I crowd under the awning at Dirty White Boy to eat the pizza. I run over to Jen for a hug and a photo op, by the time I get back to the pizza it's half gone. Oh well—the fucking tomato sauce gives me gas anyway. This chubby guy with bleached hair from New York wants drugs, and then he wants me too I think, but I don't think I'm in the mood.

Someone's after PJ too, it's the guy who's always showing off his legs from kayaking—tonight he's got cognac in a plastic cup that PJ's sipping at. The pizza's gone and Scott's fading, we get ready to head back. There's Michael and we're all in the rain together. Feels kind of good though I'm dehydrated. We're walking along and who knows what started it, but pretty soon PJ and Michael are rolling in the grass in front of one of the realtor's offices. Screaming you fucking bitch cunt—decking each other until I guess PJ's won and we're all laughing.

Pass the Boatslip and there's Colin all coked out of course, hi darling. Then the cops come by—we heard you were making a little noise—us? We're almost at Franklin, and then somehow the boy who was after me is making out with Michael. Bye girls.

Oh no there's Celebrity, luckily she's not wooing us into a k-hole, instead she's jumping into her van. The rain's getting a little—wet—we get to PJ's—bye dear. Then we speed up and by the time we're at my house we're pretty wet. I tell Scott that she sure got the grand tour tonight and she lies down on the sofa, wet clothes and all. I strip and head to the shower.

When I get out of the shower, Scott's passed out on the sofa. I squeeze a lemon in a glass of water and drink it. Know I'm not going to be able to sleep because I'm still drunk, so I get dressed again and head out. Somehow it's 3:30 already, guess I'll go to the dock because there's nowhere else to go, though I doubt anyone will be out in the rain. By this time it's kind of pouring, but I'm having fun with the hooded sweatshirt and the plastic jacket—left the umbrella at home because I'd just lose it.

I get to Commercial and up ahead there's someone—no fucking way, it's PJ out of drag and into her big red chenille sweater, rainbow flip-flops. I scream bitch turn around, she looks back and says shh, people will think we're queens. Then we're laughing all the way to the Dick Dock, underneath the fence but nope—not a soul. I'm laughing and PJ looks confused and then we're back on Commercial.

Some guy's walking down the street in shorts with no shoes, he says come up and see my lights, I've got great lights. I say how 'bout drugs, but no drugs. I start walking toward the guy's apartment and PJ says what are you doing? I say let's go see the lights. It's all the excitement we're gonna get.

We go inside and great, he's got lots of lights. Disco ball on the ceiling and then colored lights all over, he says aren't they cool? I say sure. I'm ready to go, but PJ's collapsed on the easy chair. The guy says are you horny, can I suck you're dick — I say no thanks, but can I get some water.

He comes back with two glasses of water and he's grabbing his dick, asking you're gay right? I say no kidding, and PJ's looking dazed. I'm wondering why this one weird light with a crystal base isn't on, but then somehow the guy's got PJ's dick out, he says can I suck on it and she nods. Then he's sucking PJ's dick, and PJ's making these weird faces — a cross between a duck and a sad baby.

I can't decide whether PJ's not into it at all or whether she's just uncomfortable because I'm there, so I try not to watch. Though then the guy's holding PJ's dick and saying look at this, this is a nice big dick — have you sucked this dick? I say no, PJ's making this oh-no face and then the guy's sucking again. I say take it all — take it all, and I kind of want to push his head down, but mostly I'm just laughing. Then something happens and PJ zips up her pants, says I'm ready to go.

So we're on our way, the guy wants us to stop by the Gifford House some time — okay — and then back into the rain. Now it's kind of cold. PJ says you saw my *weiner*, and we're both laughing, she says I hate sex. I say you don't have to have sex with people you're not into. She says I don't even know what I'm into anymore, I just hate sex. I say do you want a hug, and she nods her head yes—it's funny, even when she doesn't have on makeup, she moves her face like she does. Then I'm hugging PJ in the rain and we're walking home again.

DIgestion

Hot

My backpack is heavier than hell and it's 9 p.m., I always fall apart at 9. Not like I'm getting up early or anything weird — today I got up at 1 — just that between 8 and 10 I fall apart. So I'm walking out of the subway and my back is aching and the air is so thick outside I'm not sure whether I'm actually breathing. Plus there's fluid in my inner ears again, which means I can't hear anything. Usually I like to decide whether to ignore people's taunts, but now I can't hear anyone unless they're really loud, like the guy who said look at that fruity-ass nigger, hey — are you fruity? I said obviously I'm fruity, and he couldn't believe it.

I'm always the white faggot in the Latino or black or white ethnic neighborhood and everyone likes to make sure I know that. I want it to be my neighborhood too, but then I'm always leaving. A few weeks ago on the subway, a bunch of kids kept saying you like Fruit Loops or Fruity Pebbles? Then they went back and forth: I like Fruit Loops — no I like Fruity Pebbles. Pretending they were talking to each other and I wasn't even there, but of course the whole thing was about me. I was just ignoring them, but finally I said what about Skittles and everyone on the subway started laughing and the kids shut up. The ringleader even gave me this look like DAMN.

But then a week after that — on the subway again — really late this time, there was a bunch of kids — high-school kids this time (the other ones were really young). And it was just me on the subway and maybe one or two other people. And the boys just went at it, dissecting every little thing about me. I

205

wasn't even that done up, just my earrings and a purple jacket. I can't even remember what they were saying, just that I was completely drained and somehow it touched me. Nine times out of ten or maybe nineteen times out of twenty it barely grazes me, but then it'll hit hard. And that time it hit, I even glared at them — which I never do — I either ignore it or I smile. When they can tell that they've upset me, I feel like they've won.

So then the subway did some Express thing and stopped two stops further up Broadway and there I was with these two hanging plants I'd bought at the corner store, walking down Broadway in Bushwick at 3 a.m. All sketched out and angry and sick of it all and almost crying. Got home and I wanted to call someone but it was too late and I didn't know who to call.

But anyway today I'm walking out of the subway station, I get hit by a gust of wind that feels like someone just opened a huge dryer. Except it's wet heat. I can feel the sweat on my forehead. I keep thinking I can breathe, people are breathing, I can breathe. Though if the air got any thicker, who knows what would happen. I cross the street and there's that truck again, painted orange and aqua, with some business name on it, I can't remember what it's for but it almost matches the pizza place.

My backpack is way too heavy, I'm going to have to stop halfway home. There's the queen with thinning hair and painted-in eyebrows — the only other fag I've seen in the neighborhood — walking his poodle. I can tell he sees me but he's pretending not to 'cause I'm too far away so what's he to do this early? I smile and sort of wave my hand, but I've got groceries in both hands so he probably can't tell. He's talking to a woman with another poodle and he looks like he has to be engrossed. As I pass him, I say hi, how are you? His face is wide-open happy and he waves.

I'm about to pass the donut shop and I'm bracing for the rotten smell that's always outside, but luckily they've just sanded over the rancid oil by the dumpster. The streetlight's changing, so I hurry to cross, though I can feel my backpack digging into my shoulder. There's a boy across the street grabbing his dick through his pants, but just staring away and playing with something else like it's a yo-yo.

I turn, feeling the sweat pouring into my eyes, but now I've got rhythm in my legs so it's okay. I'll get home. The pink lamp shade that was on the street this morning is still there, and I want to cross and get it but I've got too much stuff. There are a bunch of guys up ahead practicing dance moves though I don't know how they can do it in this heat, shirts off though none of them are really attractive.

One of the guys looks me right in the eyes with that I-want-you-to-suck-my-dick-and-then-I'll-kill-you look; I look away. Their music's bad, but it gives me more rhythm, I'm virtually gliding by. Turn onto Lorimer and now there's sweat covering my forehead, dripping into my eyes, my whole back is sweat. Good thing I'm wearing a tank top, otherwise it would be over.

The gas station still has the American flags out from July Fourth — that was two months ago, but the gas station is Italian-owned — in the Puerto Rican section of Williamsburg, so the flags feel symbolic. I'd cut them down or replace them with Puerto Rican flags, but the gas station is open all night, all day, every day. I get up to the projects and there's one ice cream truck passing the other, two different music boxes colliding. I picture the trucks colliding too, wonder whether anyone would pay attention when it's so hot. *Everyone* would pay attention when it's so hot.

I'm so hot you could fry an egg on me. Take that back: I'm so hot you could fry tofu on me and call it an egg. Kids are playing with a hose and everyone's screaming, I'm not gonna be screaming because I've gotta get home. There's a group of four women playing cards — I'm almost home — and then from behind me someone says hi darling. I turn around to say hi, it's that sweet woman who's always friendly to me — we're neighbors — I hope she knows she just made my day.

The Regal Restaurant

I order barley soup, grape leaves, and chamomile tea. It could be that I'm worn-out or my senses are stimulated from getting fucked, but the barley soup tastes like the best thing I've ever eaten. Then "Lean on Me" comes over the radio and I start singing along softly—I can't help it—and then the women across from me are singing too. The waiter comes over and I grin; I'm embarrassed, but he says it's a beautiful song, so I keep singing. The woman facing me is wearing this great pink, orange, and yellow-striped hat and she's fully working West Coast to me, though she's New York loud and clear too. We're singing and she puts her hands up to shake her body and I'm happy and that's all, it's moments like these that save me.

Wacky Jacki's Wasabi Westaurant

I'm chewing on a piece of squash, but whoops I've scooped up an entire chunk of wasabi too — I spit it back onto the plate but my eyes are popping out with tears. I'm sweating and choking — Andee says what? Then I'm laughing laughing LAUGHING and Andee's laughing too. This woman walks by, bone-thin and pale and waspy-looking, with a jean jacket full of sewn-on square patches like she's in the Girl Scouts or something. And I'm laughing and Andee's LAUGHING and this woman walks by, she's standing up so stiff and I say to Andee there's Wacky Jackie and who knows why but that's the most hilarious thing imaginable and we can't stop.

My throat's hurting and everyone's looking at us and I'm gasping to tell Andee how Wacky Jackie traveled all over the world to get those patches: there's one for each of the different wasabis she's tried. Then she opened Wacky Jackie's Wasabi Westaurant. Andee says Wacky Jackie's Wasabi Westaurant with wasabis from all over the WORLD. In Weehawken.

And we're done for, choking and red and just about to cry... But there's more. A few days later, Andee and I are in Williamsburg and there's an empty storefront with a new canopy up. I say that's for Wacky Jackie's Wasabi Westaurant in Williamsburg, and Andee and I are falling over ourselves, stop no seriously STOP. Wacky Jackie's no Jackie O — on a warm day, with the sun shining in her eyes, she walks onward — squinting.

Van Gogh's Year

He was just confident, okay? He said I'm a painter, I don't need this damn thing anyway. Besides, the deprivation of one sense leads to the improvement of the others: Van Gogh's brush strokes swing off the canvas like centipedes in a windstorm.

Down the road a little, Van Gogh played with newts, toads, and guppies in the creek. He got in trouble for only having one year. Any convict would have known better. Sure, Van Gogh knew that Rembrandt's "Night Watch" would one day have a special security system built for it, but Japanese businessmen all over the world would hide Van Gogh in their basements.

Besides, it's Van Go*ch*, like the Hebrew letter *chet*, *l'chaim*: to life.

Digestion

The plane is going through turbulence and this guy walks towards me, crotch at my face, I'm thinking what would happen if I leaned over to take a bite? I could blame it on the turbulence, but instead I focus on eating the stir-fry I made last night. I'm not sure how well it's going to digest. I wonder if I should go into the bathroom and jerk off.

Ananda asks me if the flight attendant is straight. I say I think I saw him on *Charlie's Angels*, he's the one who replaced Cheryl Ladd's replacement. Then I remember how my sister and I got angry when Farrah Fawcett replaced Cheryl Ladd, and no one in the show seemed to notice the difference. *We* noticed Farrah's badly permed hair; Farrah's trashiness was no substitute for Cheryl's glamour.

Later, my sister and I found out that we'd been doubly duped. Because Cheryl had replaced Farrah and we'd been watching the reruns in the wrong order. After that, we stuck to *V*, where the aliens peeled off their skin to reveal the dangers of too much sun exposure. The boy behind Ananda starts pounding on the seat, I say looks like you're getting the acupressure.

I start fantasizing about having sex with someone on the plane. I picture a guy next to me with shorts on and muscular legs. I can see his hard-on pushing up at his crotch and I reach over, slowly, to put my hand on his thigh, just where the shorts end. He looks over at me. I smile. He leans over and we make out, my hand slides up his shorts to his dick, hard under boxers. My other hand is all over his chest, his hand grabbing the back of my neck. He pulls up the arm rest: gate open.

At least I had fun in Seattle, finally got to Volunteer Park early enough at night to catch the cruising. Prime time in other cities had always been 2 to 3 a.m., but in Seattle there's a sign that says the park closes at 11:30 and people actually leave. I went in one night around 10, just intending to jerk off by myself, but before I knew it, I was back the next night, sucking some guy's dick while he gave me directions.

I pulled up my shirt and someone rubbed my chest and I pulled down my pants and someone else crouched behind me, rubbing my calves while he licked my ass and I kept sucking the first guy's dick, he was wearing a baseball cap to hide his age or identity. No one seemed to notice my magenta pants or the yellow-plastic floral belt. The guy with the baseball cap was saying yeah, yeah, use your hand yeah suck that dick fuck yeah yeah fuck yeah. He grabbed my head and someone grabbed my dick, hard, and the guy rimming me stood up and pressed his dick against my ass and I angled my asshole away from him so I wouldn't suddenly be getting fucked without a condom.

I tasted precome in my mouth, the guy was ramming his dick into my throat, I grabbed his balls to push his dick in further. Yeah fuck yeah fuck oh yeah, yeah and then he came, I wanted to feel his come shooting down my throat but instead tasted it in my mouth, yum. He said thanks, zipped up and ran off; I stood up in someone's arms. Someone holding me tight and hugging me and before I had time to think about whether I should have let that guy come in my mouth, someone else was sucking my dick and the other guy was still hugging me, his tongue in my mouth, I was tasting him tasting come.

The guy sucking my dick smelled like a sex club but when he slid his lips up my shaft to my chest I almost came, rubbed his head and he started sucking fast and choking but not slowing down. I held his head still and said do you want me to come in your mouth? He nodded yes, yes, and when I came the other guy was still holding me and five guys were watching me and jerking off—maybe that was the sex club smell— and the looks in their eyes were so thankful I felt so whole and the other guy was still hugging me, yes, fucking yes—why can't it always be like this?

My grandmother Rose wants to know why all I write about is sex. The next day I was cooking vegetables in Jason's apartment where I was staying, I cut the carrots in thick diagonal chunks and put them in the steamer first. After a few minutes, I added cabbage and red onions, plus a few cloves of garlic. Then I threw in broccoli, and just before I turned off the heat, I put in snow peas and mung bean sprouts. I looked outside and there was this guy across the street, tan, with shorts and no shirt, lighting a cigarette. A few minutes later, I looked out again and there he was looking in at me like I was his wet dream. I looked him in the eyes and got hard, I looked down. I looked out and was he gone? I rushed outside in my boxers and there he was, flabbier up close, but my dick was half-hard and that's where he was looking. I said I don't live here so I can't really invite you up and the guy said oh well, looked crestfallen because this was porn, and porn is the place for crestfallen looks.

But what was really porn was when I said we can go in the laundry room and we went in, I grabbed his chest and we made out. I was so horny I went crazy with my tongue in his mouth, grabbing his ass, tasting the cigarette. And then down his stubble cheeks to his neck, bite, to his armpits, sweet, to his dick. After we came, I mixed our come into the floor and when he smiled I fell in love with the space between his teeth, he said I'll look for you. I went back to my vegetables.

When I told Jason, I think he was scandalized, he said the landlady could have walked in. I told him we were careful, even though we didn't have any laundry. When porn finally isn't boring, you can't be too careful. The next day I went jogging for the first time since Provincetown because I was craving exercise and I didn't have time to get to the gym. That's when I was really a wet dream, soaked in sweat in the park, wearing nothing but shorts and running shoes.

In the park, I was my own wet dream, which is how it should be. If I'd seen myself walking through the grass I would have gotten that shot of longing that feels so desperate I want to scream. I went into the bathroom and three guys stood shoulder-to-shoulder jerking off over the urinal except wait a minute the urinal had been removed. So much for an excuse when the cops come in. We came all over the floor, and when I walked outside I was staring at the mountains. That's what I love about Seattle. When I got back to Jason's, I noticed a streak of come that ran from the bottom of my shorts to my knee, yellow and gelatinous. Good thing no one was around. I wiped the come off and sat down to eat, food tastes so much better after exercise and sex.

Once I was good with numbers but then I learned better. Usually I prefer odd numbers, three is one of my favorites though for an odd number it's almost even. But four nervous breakdowns could easily be fourteen, so hurry, okay? Don't want to end up somewhere getting my leg amputated without anesthetic. That's from a movie, but five years ago JoAnne died from the same thing: not the leg but the lack of healthcare. In the movie, heroin was the answer — the anesthetic that came out of the junkie's pocket, magic in Bosnia — but JoAnne didn't need her leg amputated.

Five years ago feels like today, that's how I know it's a breakdown; I'm always nervous. This breakdown is like sewing, the needle goes under my skin and then I can't find it anymore. When this guy turns and stares at me, I'm checking to make sure he's cute. Not that it really matters, though if I'm going to cause a scene it might as well be a *hot* scene, he's cute, I stuff everything into his mouth. Over the urinal, of course. This is the salvation I need — his hands grabbing my chest, mouth eating me up too hard and too fast — OUCH — everyone's watching he's speaking to me in German I'm smiling in Germany I'm sucking his dick he's speaking to me in German and finally I tell him I don't speak German.

Really what I say is *ich spreche kein deutsch*, which means many different things to many different people, who I am one of. It means I'm a goddamned fucking asshole American tourist bitch who doesn't even bother to learn the languages of all the conquered lands I visit. But let's back up a bit, this is Germany not Panama, okay? This is the country where *ich bin Jüde,* covering a window overlooking the River Spree, is still a political statement, and I'm Jewish too. This is the country where, Andee says, there are so many fascists and what can you do with them because they can't be educated and you can't just shoot them all.

I'm trying to remember where that joke comes from, though when Andee says it he's serious, daring me to respond. The guy who's speaking understands *ich spreche kein deutsch* to mean translate what you just said to me, to the beat of a drum. I want to kiss you. I want to lick you all over. I want to suck your dick. I want to fuck you. I want you to fuck me.

At least he didn't say man you've got my crank dripping spooge, buddy I wanna suck your fat cock man I wanna drive my tool through that boypussy dude I'm gonna nut all over your face and then buddy I want you to throw me up against the wall and fuck me like the bitch I am, *man.* That would have taken too long. I'm already ducking, sucking his dick: this is where I was meant to be, I'm so hungry.

But then he's asking me to leave the world of the urinal, the world I know and love, for his translated sex talk, induced by ecstasy and aggravated by speed. Stop watering the plants and feed me. He wants to know what I'm on, I'm on Candid Camera, snap snap. He can't believe I'm not high, you're a really horny guy, what do you want — anything you want. He takes out a bag of pills and vials and my eyes go wide, later I'll learn drugs are cheap here, twelve marks for a hit of e — that's five dollars — but for now my eyes go wide. I say I'm okay. I'm not okay.

Then I'm trying to leave but my bag is gone;

it's an easy nervous breakdown, textbook definition: passport, driver's license, credit cards, ATM cards, phone cards, purple nylon jacket that's almost my trademark, French-cuffed blue shirt that I wear with everything, dark green sweater that fits better than the bright green one that's in New York anyway, money, Fisherman's Friend throat lozenges, the case I keep my earrings in, my journal, German phrase book, Berlin gay guide, Berlin map, new backpack, toothpicks and a lifetime of empty promises—wait that's not gone, why couldn't someone have stolen what I don't need?

Here's where the irony comes in, an ingredient in it's own right—as they say in so-called democratic countries. I've been to countless clubs in New York and San Francisco and Seattle and Boston and wherever the fuck else I've been, stashed my bag in countless corners and on countless stages and under countless sofas and never once was it taken from me... Well, maybe once, but anyway here I am in Berlin, where I could probably leave my bag in a park and find it the next day, wait let's not exaggerate but Berlin is safer than the richest areas of most U.S. suburbs.

Let's back up to the day after I arrive in Berlin: Prenzlauerberg where they still use coal stoves, darkening the buildings but it's warm out—I shouldn't get ahead of myself. It's sunny and warm, I go jogging but why is everybody staring? The second day they're pointing too—it's because I'm not wearing a shirt and that's when I know I'm in Germany: they've got naked men on billboards but it's against the rules to jog shirtless. Andee says people don't display themselves like that here, but then Jens, Andee's German boyfriend, says Andee's more German than the Germans. Even though Andee's only been in Berlin for a year, he already wants me to think I'm wrong.

In Andee's America, there are shirtless men on every corner waiting to pump me up with steroids disguised as vitamins. These are the men I hate to want, when I get tendinitis it's hard not to need vitamins. I only wish Andee wouldn't say America when he means the U.S., America's more than thirty countries where neither of us have ever been.

I know about overprocessing: in seventh grade, Zelda Alpern put Clorox in her hair. It turned white and then fell out. But it looked hot, I'd leave peroxide in my hair all day but it just turned orange. Until I discovered Ultra Blue, which wasn't just my mood but my hair bleach too.

But back to the bag of drugs: this time I don't want to get high, just want the adventure of people I'll soon hate becoming my closest friends for a few hours. Four days on the verge of collapse in exchange for: four days on the verge of collapse. Sometimes it seems like an even trade.

But this time my bag's gone and my bathroom lover has moved on to easier prey. I'm half-naked and wet—sweat—and it's forty degrees outside, how far to the nearest cab? Luckily I find Maraîke, the nice one at the coatcheck, who shines her flashlight onto each bag until every single one refuses to transform itself into mine. Then she guides me to the bar, her ecstasy's definitely kicking in, she gives me her clothes. We exchange numbers and then I'm out the door, it's 7 a.m. and I'm not nearly as cold as I could have been.

Where I'm staying they're sure cold and Andee says you're too friendly, have to act cold too because that's what they understand. Germans think Americans are friendly on the outside but there's nothing underneath. Andee knows that Americans might be friendly on the outside, but they're vicious monsters underneath. The next day Andee tells me to extend myself, ask them out, not the monsters but the people who are supposedly hosting me. Andee says this is how wars start. Of course he's right.

I don't want to go to war with Andee, who says he likes the Marxist influence here but wait there are no Marxists; of course it rains all the time like Seattle except really it's sunny only grey. The '60s modern architecture is enough to make Andee swoon. He's showing me his new potbelly, after years of being too skinny. He plays with his new fat like Silly Putty.

There are things I remember even though I've never tried to forget: in tenth grade, Rebecca Tushnet wrote about the taste of blood in her mouth like metal. Which reminds me of one of my last nights in Provincetown, on the dock of course. Someone had just fucked my mouth so hard that I was bleeding because of his cockring — metal — and then this preppy boy showed up. I dove right for his dick, thinking the blood was only between my upper teeth and the gums so this was still kind of safe, the guy said you want me to fuck that ass don't you.

The porn talk was almost cute because the guy was so nervous about it. I wanted everything: his dick in my ass, his come in my mouth mixing with the blood. Let's not exaggerate the blood, gushing onto the sand and forming rivers of sentiment. That's everything? Okay: he throws me against the wall, pulls down my pants and shoves his cock in my ass, just like the rape scene in Todd Haynes' *Poison* except outdoors instead of in jail—watching *Poison* was the first time I ever really wanted to get fucked. He puts me in a headlock and then fucks me until he comes in my ass NO mouth and then we're rolling in the sand with pants down and midsections—that's cock, stomach, thighs—exposed I grind my dick into his chest until I shoot in bursts that go all the way up his nose and into his brain. He chokes, on my tongue: everything.

When Andee says *you are sex* it's not like that, we have to be clear here; he's not talking about the S tattooed on my chest, blue and red arms in a tribal-block pattern wait it's anime no it's just a sweet sweatsuit okay—I'm not running shirtless through Berlin because the Kryptonite gave me tendinitis. But shame on Andee, if anyone should know then he should know I'd be Wonderwoman; with the tendinitis gone I could wear those bracelets again.

Despite my Superhero status, Andee wants to get into drama on the subway. After two weeks, my jetlag is finally ending and my bronchitis is just beginning, an ode to all the smokers in Berlin. Andee wants to know if there's anything he could be doing. We've had this conversation too many times. Andee and I have had nervous breakdowns together and apart, moved cross-country together and apart, and here we are in Berlin, together and apart. Still he can't hug me. I say I'm glad you have Jens, fucking Jens means you touch him even when you're not fucking. Sure, I'm touched but will you ever touch me?

Here's the important part: Andee hugs me. It's not like the preppy boy in Provincetown who should never have been my dreamboy, coming all over my chest and then leaving, even though both of us wanted what most people call more: a bed and some time alone. For all these years, Andee's been getting bags under his eyes worrying that's what I wanted from him, a bed or something more. I can't believe it: he hugs me. It's not a big deal, it's a hug goodbye it's not a big deal it's what I want it's not a big deal...

Andee notices when the West German fags posing as Americans are drunk enough for their internalized homophobia to go down: they're cruising me, especially the one with the backwards baseball cap, UConn Lacrosse t-shirt. I'm amused and Andee's getting his shotgun ready, he can shoot a bug on a wall because he grew up in Montana. His brother owns five guns, though they're at his mother's house while his brother teaches elementary school in Palm Springs.

But this story has a happy ending: it's not just a surveillance camera recording me as I examine myself in the mirror to see if I'm disappearing. I'm back at the club where I lost my bag, but this time the music is even better; dancing I get so centered that I'm on a swing set, swinging higher and higher as my body plants itself deeper into the ground: a young tree. I go in the backroom to take a break. Nothing's going on until I stretch my dick into this butch guy's mouth and then quickly I fold myself onto another guy so that I can suck a third guy's dick: I'm Mary Lou Retton with longer legs, no Wheaties necessary. It's a fourth guy I'm crazed for, fly unbuttoned into the third guy's mouth until the third guy needs a break.

Now's my chance, but what is it about this new guy that makes me crazy? Really I'm too crazy to think about it, he's crazy too and pretty soon I've got his dick in my mouth, and sure someone else is trying to fuck me, but my attention is on the new guy's sweat as he bends over to suck my dick. I'm rubbing his chest then standing up to grab him, his ass, his neck, all of him, his wet wet tongue into my mouth and then he's spitting on my face, wow I'm spitting at him but it goes into his hair because I'm taller, I rub it in.

I pull him onto me, falling into everybody else's laps. Bones don't break but I think about it. I'm just everywhere that's here, with him; I want to say something but I don't want to speak English, his cock into my mouth again, he's trying to come but not in my mouth and I'm trying to get him to come in my mouth before I come. He's shoving his dick in and out then jerking off then in and out, my finger into his asshole. I'm rubbing his chest full of sweat and he spits on me again, I want more and more and more spit and sweat, a bubbly sweet glistening mess that's both of us and finally he's ready to add to it, moaning and shaking come all over my neck. I almost feel it go into my veins, of course that's possible. Standing up, I come onto his chest, rub him all over me, help him back into his pants. I'm kissing him and then he's gone, I'm back on the dance floor until I'm about to fall over and that's when I leave.

Sure, tomorrow my head will feel like there are sharks swimming in it and the next day I'll be sick again, but this story has a happy ending. Andee's modeling for me, pulling up his shirt again. He squeezes his fat into a new shape: look honey I'm pregnant!

Mattilda, a.k.a. Matt Bernstein Sycamore, is the editor of *Tricks and Treats: Sex Workers Write About Their Clients* (Haworth 2000) and *Dangerous Families: Queer Writing on Surviving* (Haworth 2003). This is his first novel. His writing has been widely published, in places as diverse as *Best American Erotica*, *Best American Gay Fiction*, *Women and Performance*, and *Slingshot*. He is an instigator of Gay Shame: the Virus in the System, the radical queer activist group that celebrates resistance by fighting the monster of assimilation. He lives in San Francisco, where he is at work on a new anthology, *Resisting Assimilation: Alternatives to the Gay Mainstream*, and a second novel. His web address: www.mattbernsteinsycamore.com.